Saving Sophia

Neonatal surgery, blisters, and bliss, on the rocky road to motherhood

Caro Feely

www.CaroFeely.com

SAVING SOPHIA

Copyright © 2023 by Caro Feely

Also By

In the Vineyard Series:
Grape Expectations
Saving Our Skins
Vineyard Confessions (previously titled 'Glass Half Full')
Cultivating Change

Prequel to the Vineyard Series:
Saving Sophia (this book)

Non-fiction
Wine, the Essential Guide

About Caro Feely

Caro traded in her life as an IT Strategy Consultant to pursue her dreams. She is author of six books and writes a regular wine column for Living, a magazine about France. Along with writing books she runs an organic estate with wine school, yoga school, and accommodation, in South-West France with her partner, Sean. She's an acclaimed writer, an accredited wine educator, a registered yoga teacher, a confident and engaging speaker and an experienced event facilitator. Follow Caro by joining her newsletter at www.carofeely.com and connecting at www.instagram.com/carofeely or via the social media network links below.

instagram.com/carofeely

facebook.com/caro.feely.wines/

linkedin.com/carow

amazon.com/author/carofeely

goodreads.com/author/show/6176029.Caro_Feely

Note from the Author

This book is memoir. It reflects my recollections of experiences over time. Some names and characteristics have been changed, some events have been compressed or changed, and dialogue has been recreated. Thank you for joining me on this journey.

Contents

For Sophia.

Gratitude

My deepest gratitude to the people of Temple Street Children's University Hospital, Prof. Puri, the Domino programme midwives of the National Maternity Hospital, Dublin, my friend Aideen Dunne, our families, and to the generous, loving people that supported us, and prayed for Sophia.

My hope for this story:

May this book inspire you to check in on a friend that is a new mum or a work colleague on maternity leave, to hug a tree, and to cultivate wonder at the miracle of life. Our world is filled with magic. The act of breathing is a love story with this earth, the trees breathing out and you breathing in, you breathing out and the trees breathing in, all connected. In this time of the environmental crisis, we are extraordinarily alive, each of us players in taking on this challenge and bringing forth change.

Prologue

The paediatrician came back without our baby.

'I'm afraid we have a problem,' he said.

Stars bounced around my vision of the Doctor's talking head, his voice far away like a dream. I felt like I was sinking into a void. We had experienced the deepest, most life affirming event the night before, the birth of our first child. Now she was being taken away. It was a moment that would take us on an intense journey and change the course of our lives.

Part 1: Love

'We were together. I forget the rest.'

Walt Whitman[i]

Or more aptly for this story: We were together. I remember everything.

[i] *This quote is a paraphrased rendition of a quote from Walt Whitman's 1855 self-published collection of poems, 'Leaves of Grass'. The actual quote 'we were together— all else has long been forgotten by me', appears in the poem called 'Once I pass'd through a populous city' page 94.*

Chapter One

Two sides of the sea

It was a time of extremes, stark in its ferocious joy and fear, in its awakening to the deepest meaning of love, life, and home. Love, a connection to a being that goes beyond romance and reaches into your soul. Life, a vibration that goes beyond a body, an energy to celebrate, and to powerfully pray for. Home, something beyond a house, where we are with our family, in the largest sense.

Although this story happened two decades ago, it's as clear as yesterday. I returned home after a week away, dropped my travel bag inside the front door then walked through the kitchen out into the garden to where I knew Sean would be. White blush roses contrasted with freshly dug vegetable beds. He was at the back near the shed, his skin bright with a sheen of perspiration from turning the compost heap. Aromas of earth and sea interspersed with his smell as we embraced.

'I missed you.'

'I missed you too,' I replied, giving his smooth, tanned arm a squeeze, before stepping away. I was loath to let go but needed to allow him space to continue his task.

'It feels like wine time,' I said after a moment of stillness.

'Good idea, I'm almost finished. There's a bottle of Sauvignon in the fridge.'

In the kitchen, I opened the bottle, enjoying the pop of the cork, and the sound of the liquid pouring into the glasses. We were wine lovers. Sean's grandparents had been winegrowers, and we had a dream to go wine farming in France one day. Sean followed a weekly night class in wine, and I followed one to learn French.

Back outside, I rested the glasses against a log, then swept leaves off the garden chairs and sat down. Sean placed his spade on the heap and joined me, his body moving easily and confidently after the effort. We clinked cheers, then sipped, savouring the fresh citrus and grassy notes that matched the spring day.

I recounted my trip, a week in London to assess an internet start-up, followed by visiting friends in Oxford, where I met their son for the first time. Before he was born, we saw them regularly, over to party in Dublin for the weekend. It was strange to see them with a child, less footloose, but thriving. As we picnicked on the river beside Oxford university, I asked, 'What made you leap in?'

Without explanation Bev knew I was asking about starting a family not having a swim. She hugged her son, all blond curls and cherubic, then let him go.

'I wanted to experience the deepest love,' she said.

The deepest love. Years before, my sister Foo and I, had agreed we didn't want children. They kept you awake, were demanding, and OMG those nappies. If that wasn't enough, they became toxic when they hit adolescence. I knew first-hand from how I behaved as a teenager.

Foo and I watched the film 'Antonia's Line' together.

'So that's why people have children: it's a way to live forever through your descendants,' I said. At the time I couldn't see any other reasons. Now I added 'deepest love'.

The idea of having children frightened me. Total disruption and sleepless nights didn't fit my career-focused life. Our best friends' son was the first baby I met close up. He was six weeks old when Aideen and Barry collected me from the airport the day I touched down in Dublin for the first time. That weekend they invited me to their house for the day.

'Do you want to hold him?' asked Aideen.

I was scared, petrified of this tiny being that could cry the house down, but I said yes. Holding him close, feeling his eagerness for life bursting out in constant movement, seeing the love that came with raising a family, opened a door into my heart. Aideen and Barry successfully balanced careers and children. Mike and Bev, our friends in Oxford, were handling it like pros, and they were far from grandparents and siblings as we would be.

My maternal instinct woke up. What meeting Aideen and Barry's baby started, Mike and Bev's toddler completed; a transformation of the 'no kids' me, into a person that wanted to have children. Sean had always wanted children. Now I had returned from Oxford on the same page as him and bursting with excitement.

'So, there you go. That was my 'Road to Damascus' experience this weekend,' I said. 'I want to have kids.'

I expected him to be delighted, thrilled, ready to race upstairs to see what we could do about it. Instead, he gave me a worried look.

'I wanted kids before. Now I'm not so sure. I'm still doing the CFA. Look at the long hours we work. How will a baby fit into our lives?'

Sean was senior writer for an investment bank. In addition to a hefty workload, he was studying to become a Chartered Financial Analyst (CFA) and was in his third and final year of the challenging course. It was important for his career and a major time commitment. I understood his reticence. We were opposites again. I was saying yes, he was saying no. We were like that. He said black, I said white.

'But if we don't do it now, we'll never do it,' I said.

'Even if we want them, are we ready for it?' asked Sean.

'There's never a perfect time. Do you really want a life without kids? I think we'll regret it if we don't have them.'

'Perhaps we should wait another year or two,' he replied.

'I'm nearly thirty-four. If we wait, we're into the high-risk zone. Past thirty-five the risk of things like Down syndrome increases exponentially. If we're going to do it, we have to do it now.'

I left the threats of waiting hanging in the air between us for a moment.

'Plus, we don't know how long it will take. Maybe I won't fall pregnant straight away,' I added. 'That makes it even more urgent.'

We exchanged a look of complicity.

'Right so. That's decided,' said Sean.

We clinked glasses. Our garden chairs, hand-me-downs from Sean's parents, were perfectly angled for the late afternoon rays. They had travelled from Pietermaritzburg to Johannesburg to Cape Town to Dublin. They had history and longevity, and delicately peeling green paint to prove it. Beside them, a bench that Sean had made from a gnarled tree trunk, cosied up against the garden shed.

'Tell me more about Mike and Bev,' said Sean.

We had known each other a long time. Mike shared a house with me at university and Bev was Mike's best friend. When Sean and I moved to Cape Town they took us in for a few months while we looked for a place to live. The care of our friends floated through my mind as we chatted. Memories of our life in South Africa washed over me.

Sean was my soulmate. We met a decade before. I heard his suave voice behind me in a tutorial, turned, and was hit with a powerful dose of love at first sight. My core fizzed. He was tall with long, honey-blond, wavy hair, and a quiet confidence that came from being a journalist, someone who talked with ministers of parliament, CEOs, and rebel leaders daily. I would discover that he was creative, alternative, smart, and kind. South Africa was in transition, Nelson Mandela was free at last, and the country was heading for the first real elections. It was an exciting time to be a journalist.

We were both working in Johannesburg and doing a post graduate degree in Economics by distance learning. At the on-campus study day where we met, I talked to Sean every moment I could. We sat next to each other at lunch. At afternoon tea, we discussed meeting to work on tutorials together, but at the end of the day, he left without saying goodbye or giving me his card. I ran after him and caught up as he closed his car door, scribbled my home number on a piece of paper and passed it through the window, smiling. Months later when he called, he had to remind me who he was. He had taken too long. We started a phase of 'we're just friends' but we knew we wanted more.

That summer we fell in love. It wasn't the fizzy, love at first sight, that I had felt when we met. It was a deep love, founded on tea shared in bed before dawn, sunrise swims, and nightly debates on philosophy, politics, and economics. We got to know each other's minds and bodies, the pure joy of being together. I was so in love I regularly forgot my handbag in restaurants after we had dined. I was smitten. In one of the most dangerous and crime ridden cities in the world, I never lost it. The restaurant staff would announce they had the bag and hand it over with a smile that said 'starstruck lover'.

That October, Sean was part of the press team that accompanied Nelson Mandela on his first trip to address the United Nations and the World Bank. There were no mobile phones or reminder apps and he remembered to call me for my birthday. That's when I knew our relationship was more than fizzy love.

Now we were ten years on, in a different hemisphere, preparing to embark on the next phase of our love story. Sean's arm touched mine. I felt electricity between us, chemistry magic that couldn't be explained. Sean leaned in and our lips brushed together, then we kissed, a deep kiss of lovers hungry for more. I suggested the thick mat of spring grass would be perfect, Sean countered that our garden was overlooked by neighbours. Hands locked together; we went inside to work on our new mission.

The following weekend the cold air slapped my face alive as we raced past the Killiney DART (the abbreviation for 'Dublin Area Rapid Transit') station, revelling in the speed of our bikes. The other side of the train track, waves knocked seaweed and plastic debris along the beach, up and back, up and back. I freewheeled for a moment, my lungs filling with air laced with iodine aromas, and joy bubbling inside me. A backward glance revealed Sean grinning as he closed the gap between us. I picked up my pedals again and turned my bike away from the sea as I geared down. Halfway up I got off to push. Sean passed me, legs pumping.

'Faster! Faster!' He yelled and broke into laughter.

'Wait for me!' I shouted.

Sean had been riding his bike back from work every day for months. He was bike fit. That's why he was beating me. I smiled at myself finding excuses but didn't try to catch him. My legs were jelly, and we weren't even halfway. At the top of the hill, I climbed back on and pedalled like mad to catch up. On Vico Road, the vista over Killiney Bay was so good I forgot the race, dropped my feet off the pedals and drenched my senses in it as I rolled effortlessly down the hill. I caught up with Sean where sea splendour flashed between houses and through parallel windows. At a perfect gap we stopped, the framed view too good to dash past. The sun lit the water, all shimmer around Dalkey Island, then skittered behind a cloud and everything changed colour.

Another short burst and we were at Sandycove. A huddle of stalwart swimmers gathered on the lane to the

'Forty Foot', a favourite outdoor bathing place. I was sorry I didn't have togs with me or time to spare. Our destination, a seafood-shop built on one of the piers of Dun Laoghaire's harbour, was calling.

The building was grey and solid, the air around it thick with the smell of fish. Seals played lazily in the water, waiting for off-cuts from women filleting and preparing the bounty. We took our time looking at the selection, then settled for a bag of mackerel. Fish firmly strapped to Sean's handlebars, we turned for home.

At Bullock Harbour more seals provided an excuse for a break. The screech of gulls and smells of seaweed and boat oil assaulted our senses. The place was buzzing; a couple prepared a small boat to go fishing and another group wrestled kayaks into the water. Next to us, a tall redhead unloaded more kayaks from a van. Intrigued, I moved closer.

'Hello,' I said. 'How far do you go?'

He looked up, surprised by the interruption.

'It depends. For beginners like this, if the conditions are good, we might go to Greystones. I could go around the whole island of Ireland.'

He said it matter of fact, it was the way it was, there was no swagger in it.

'I would love to see the coast from the sea. How long would it take to be good enough to go from Bullock to Greystones?'

'One weekend. Some of these punters never paddled a kayak before yesterday.'

He smiled and introduced himself, then dug into the van cab for a business card. On it was written 'Redhead

Rob, Kayaker of Note'. Actually, it was something else, but that's what it should have said.

'We run these weekends every month or so. Why don't you come and try it out?'

'Thanks,' I said. 'Maybe we will.'

A member of Rob's group mounted a kayak with great care. He didn't look confident enough to get out of the harbour, let alone to Greystones. Soon he was joined by others including the red-headed leader. They loped out to sea in an elongated posse. We watched a while, then carried on, snatching glimpses of them between the houses as we went.

On the last uphill stretch, I stopped to give my legs a break. Killiney Hill stretched above me, and below, a scrabble of rocks and grass descended to cliffs and White Rock beach. Out on the open sea, the kayakers started their traverse of the bay. How brave they looked, striking out across the water in their tiny vessels. I felt a tinge of nerves for them, but it was calm; they had picked a good day. Even without kayakers to watch, I never tired of that view, sea and sky in constant flux of tides and time. They were halfway across the bay when I climbed back on the bike. Sean was waiting at the top.

'Where were you? I had almost given up,' he said.

'I was watching the kayakers. Maybe we should do it.'

'Maybe,' said Sean. 'Let's find out more about it. Ready for the fun part?'

'Ready!'

We raced down Strathmore Road, fish bag flapping, a long shout of 'wheeeee', and past the DART station for home.

A few weeks later, it was us kitted out in wetsuits preparing to launch kayaks in Bullock Harbour. The morning before, I had never been in a kayak. Now, after a day learning basics in a pool in Wicklow, I was ready for the open sea.

Sean and I lived in a semi-detached house five minutes' walk from the Shankill end of Killiney Beach. A weekend wasn't a weekend without a couple of hours running, walking, or biking in the biting winter wind or brisk summer breeze that came off the sea. Right then, looking at the white horses, I felt scared of it. Seeing the flash of uncertainty in me, Rob shouted, 'Don't worry Caro, you'll handle it. It's calm enough for beginners.'

Remembering how timid the rookie looked getting into his kayak, I tried to do it nonchalantly. My kayak rocked, I almost kissed the water but righted it and stayed miraculously dry. Gripping my paddle, I wobbled out of the harbour determined to stay on. Sean cruised in beside me, paddling with ease, and Rob shouted encouragement from behind.

Out on the open water I paused a moment to look back to land. Sea crashed onto barnacle encrusted rocks, and birds rose and fell with the waves in search of food. There was a mesmerising wildness that was unimaginable from the land side of this place. Gulls, terns, and oystercatchers floated into the air, then settled back, following the ocean like a breath. I could have watched the seabirds and their dance for hours; but on seeing how far ahead the first group was, I got down to the business of paddling. My competitive streak rose, and I pulled hard despite the ache in my arms from practice in the pool the day before. The kayak sped up and my confidence grew with each stroke. A few minutes later Rob drew in next to me.

'You're doing well Caro. Don't overdo it. There's a long way to go. Don't feel you have to keep up. I'll stay back if you need a breather.'

Near Dalkey Island the 'fluk fluk' sound of our paddles slowed. I braked, then watched the drops on my airborne paddle free fall back to the sea. A fizz snaked across the water and a seal's head popped out. We paused.

Rob lobbed a small ball to him. The seal caught it, balanced it on his nose, threw it up and caught it again. He kept playing, offering an impromptu show. I called a walk where you met unexpected wildlife a 'magic walk'. This was a 'magic kayak'. Eventually the seal got bored and let Rob retrieve his ball.

We floated to shore on the current and parked on a small beach on the northwest end to take a walk around. A feral black billy goat stepped out above us, his round-horns held high, surprised at finding intruders on his island home. He looked proud. I would have been proud too: Dalkey Island was a wild beauty. The only scars were mounds of litter outside and inside the round Martello tower near the centre.

'The wind's getting up, we'd better get on,' shouted Rob.

We followed him back to the beach, pushed out, and then mounted our kayaks. The members of the other group, all experienced kayakers, took the outside passage where large rollers crashed onto the island. Sean, Rob, and I took the safer inside passage where white horses played.

Out on the open sea the swell looked exuberant. I felt a jab of adrenalin.

Our two groups connected back together near Dalkey Head, then struck out across Killiney Bay. I remembered how the kayakers had looked from up on Vico Road. Now we were the brave ones out on the water.

My arms hurt. In more open sea the wind was stronger and the waves too. I felt myself lagging. Rob shouted encouragement.

'We're more than halfway! You're doing great!'

I nodded, mind and body focussed on staying right side up and moving forward.

Near Bray Head the sea boiled with the meeting of waves coming from opposite sides of the point. I kept paddling, rode successfully through it, and felt a thrill at having made it. As I basked in my success a wave hit me side-on. In the moment of inattention my body balance wasn't ready. My kayak flipped. I was underwater.

I tried to flip back using the technique I had learnt in the pool. It didn't work. I tried again and felt a twinge of panic. After the third fail I knew I had to get out of the kayak and head for the surface. I needed air. I grabbed the sides and pushed outwards with all my power. I was stuck. I pushed again. The panic gave way to calmness, a feeling of going into a long tunnel. Something roused me and I gave another yank. I spun out and away wondering which way to turn, then remembered to look for light, saw it and kicked frantically towards it. A second later I smashed through the surface and gasped glorious cold air. Clinging to my kayak like a limpet, I hung there, drawing deep life-saving breaths as adrenalin raced through my body. Rob sped towards me. He was one with his boat: it was like an extension of him, a body part. He righted my kayak and helped me back in.

I felt like giving up, but there was no easy beach nearby, just tall cliffs with waves crashing onto their jagged faces. Feeling even more respect for the sea, the beauty of the raging seascape was lost on me for the rest of the journey. It seemed harmless at the time. In fifteen minutes, I was back on land with what appeared to be no ill effects.

CHAPTER TWO

Aliens in the time of gardening

I was an alien with an Alien Book to prove it. Every year I went to the Alien's Office on Harcourt Street to renew my licence to be one. A year before, a new law had been passed, requiring my Irish passport holding partner to accompany me. Sean wasn't pleased but I was. Queueing alone on a cold, dark street, was worse than together.

The expedition was like a pre-dawn camping trip. Our equipment included serious outdoor clothes, fold up chairs, and a basket of biscuits and tea. That morning we were first in the queue. We flipped a coin to see who would have their turn in the car first. I lost. Sean left me and tucked himself under a blanket in the passenger seat. He waved, then put the seat back, and closed his eyes. I gripped my hands around a warm mug of tea and settled in for the long wait. A few minutes later, a car pulled in behind ours. A couple got out and took the spot behind me.

'I see you come prepared,' said the tall, dark-haired man, in a soft Wexford accent.

'Old hands,' I replied.

He laughed.

'I'm Caro. That's Sean,' I said pointing. 'He went to warm up. We take turns.'

'That's a good idea in this cold. I'm Andrew, and this is Penny,' he said.

'Same car,' said Penny with a wide smile, and an American accent that explained why they were there. We compared Rovers, ours green, theirs blue.

'Can I offer you some tea? A biscuit?' I asked.

'If you have enough to spare,' replied Andrew.

'Plenty,' I said. 'But only one extra cup.'

'That's perfect. We'll share.'

I poured and passed the biscuits. Sean, seeing a street party developing, came to join us.

'So, what brings you fine folks to Dublin?' asked Andrew, after a round of introductions.

'Work at first. But we both have Irish roots. Sean has an Irish passport,' I said.

'I was born in South Africa, but my gran registered me as a foreign birth. She spoke a lot about Ireland. She wanted us to remember our roots,' said Sean.

'Cheers to your grandmother,' said Penny, lifting the tea, and taking a sip.

'I always wanted to come to Ireland,' added Sean. 'After university, I looked for a job here but there was nothing. It was before the Celtic Tiger. I landed up working in the

UK as a security guard instead. I'd never been to Ireland before Caro got a project here.'

'I'd visited Castletownsend in County Cork working as an *au pair* on my year of working my way around the world. I couldn't understand what people were saying. The strong west Cork accent had me baffled,' I said.

'I know that feeling,' replied Penny, laughing.

'When I got the project in Dublin a few years ago my Irish colleagues made me feel so welcome. Sean came over to see me two months into the project and it already felt like home for me. We took a drive out west, to Galway and Clifden. The landscapes were dramatic, and people were so friendly. We were smitten. A few months later my company offered me a permanent move. We loved Cape Town, but we had come to love Dublin too. We spent many hours debating the pros and cons. In the end, we decided it was too good of an opportunity to miss. With an Irish passport Sean could look for work without any problems.'

'That's a big plus,' said Penny.

'You're so right, for him and for me. Later, when I wanted to move jobs, it was thanks to my Irish husband that I could do it, otherwise I would have had to stay with the company that organised my work permit. Sean accompanying his alien came in useful.'

'Ah, so that's how it is,' said Andrew.

'Andrew's doing the same for me,' said Penny. 'Chaperone services.'

We laughed. Penny had a way of expressing things that was hilarious. She was a natural comedian.

'We moved to Ireland thinking it would be a couple of years. It's already four. We love it here,' I said.

'Wow, four years of queueing. Sounds like a lifetime. This is only our second time,' said Penny.

'I've got used to it. Not that I want to stay an alien. As soon as I can apply for an Irish passport, I will,' I said.

'The word "alien" is so funny. Don't you just love our green book?' asked Penny. 'Sometimes I really do feel like an alien. I walk into a shop and the salesperson keeps chatting to her friend like I'm invisible. And even when I ask a question, I'm ignored. Maybe I'm an invisible alien.'

We cracked up. For an American, European customer service could feel like dis-service.

We were laughing, but it is worth pausing, to consider what alien means. 'Alien' in the etymological sense is rooted in the Latin *alienus*, 'belonging to another'. We have also come to understand it in the astrophysical sense, as in 'from another planet', 'not human'. It's a word that reinforces a sense of otherness, of not belonging, for someone new to a place. The word made me feel unwelcome. But Irish people made me feel welcome.

We had both travelled and lived abroad before and been exposed to diverse cultures. Despite my Alien Book, Ireland was the place we felt most welcomed, most at home, of all the places we visited on our travels. Perhaps it was something in our atoms. Sean's grandparents on both sides, hailed from Ireland. I had a great grandparent on each side that was Irish. Nonetheless, I was deeply South African, some of my roots there went back six generations. Mostly I think it was the people. Amazing people like my colleagues and friends, Aideen and Barry, that had welcomed us with open arms. When someone asked me where I was from, I would reply with our Dublin neighbourhood.

'No, I mean, where are you from, your accent?' they would say. The question always came as a surprise. I didn't feel 'other' or foreign. I didn't feel alien, despite what the green book said. I loved Ireland for that. There was a kindness in people that you didn't find as easily elsewhere.

Penny was on a roll, she regaled us with stories. We laughed so much the growing queue wondered what we were up to. Andrew was a pilot; they had met in the USA, and he had talked Penny into coming home to Ireland when the Celtic Tiger started to roar. They came back via London where Penny had a great job with the BBC. She missed her work in London. Like Sean, when he looked for a journalist position in Dublin, she found the Irish media was a closed shop, difficult, if not impossible, to enter.

'So, where do you live?' I asked.

'Swords,' replied Andrew.

'Ah da Northside, no fancy delis over there,' I joked. There was a Northside Southside divide in Dublin that came up regularly in comedians' skits.

'It's close to the airport,' said Andrew defensively.

'There's that,' I laughed again, teasing him. 'We lived on the Northside. It was like another planet compared to the Southside. We saw more crime there than in Johannesburg.'

'Ah come now,' said Andrew.

'Seriously!' replied Sean. 'We saw our neighbour's apartment being burgled, we called the *Gardaí* and they said, 'Is anyone in danger?' We said 'No', and they said, 'Ah well, it's not that urgent then'. They arrived an hour later. The thieves were long gone.'

An Garda Síochána is the Irish police force, 'the Guardians of the Peace', commonly referred to as the *Gardaí* or 'the Guards'.

'That's not all,' continued Sean. 'A year later our buzzer rang at seven on a Sunday morning. A voice on the intercom said, 'It's special agent Ryan of the *Gardaí*. We need you to let us into the apartment block.' It was a guy we had seen on the news the night before, the chief investigator of a drug-trafficking murder where the victim was thrown into the canal. He flashed his badge and I let them in. They waited until I was back upstairs with our door locked then we heard them smash their way into the downstairs apartment. A while later, they left with a man with his hands cuffed, and his head covered.'

'No way!' exclaimed Penny. 'It sounds like you two attract some *interesting* stuff. I'm not sure it's safe to be around you.'

We laughed. The morning's alien outing was turning out to be more fun than we expected.

'When we arrived, our nearest food shop on the Northside hadn't heard of feta. On the Southside, the local shop had it. There's a deli in Glasthule that has a great gourmet selection. The only thing I haven't found is fresh figs, I love them.'

'My parents have a fig tree in their garden down in Wexford,' said Andrew.

'Wow!' I said. 'I didn't know figs could grow in Ireland.'

'Theirs does well. We get figs every year. It's protected against a warm, south-facing wall. That probably helps. Next time I go down, I'll get you a cutting.'

'Thanks Andrew, I'd love that,' I said.

Sean had planted grape vines and Irish heritage apple trees in our garden, now we would complement them with a fig acclimatised to Irish weather. The morning was turning out to be more than fun.

'Did you say Wexford, Andrew?' asked Sean. 'My grandparents were from New Ross.'

'I grew up in Enniscorthy, about half an hour from New Ross,' said Andrew.

That set the two of them off on a 'Wexford love' exchange, for about a quarter of an hour. The queue filled in cadence with the emptying of the thermos. By dawn, it snaked down Harcourt Street and Penny and Andrew felt like old friends.

By the time the Alien's Registration Office opened its doors, we had agreed to meet for dinner and exchanged contact details. The seeds of friendship had been sown.

A couple of weeks later at a bistro on Merrion Row, it was obvious Penny was pregnant, she must have already been when we met in the Aliens' queue. We congratulated them heartily.

When the wine arrived, Penny said 'no wine for me' in a martyr tone. We laughed. I was struck again by how she could make simple statements funny. I added 'no wine' to the cons of pregnancy. As a confirmed wine lover it was a big con for me, but not enough to put me off. We were too far into the idea of starting a family. Seeing these new friends start their baby journey made me even keener.

At the end of the evening, Andrew handed over the promised fig cutting. The following day, we dug a deep hole in the garden and settled the fig in next to a south facing wall a good distance from the house. We read that the roots of fig trees were extensive and strong, they could upset foundations. Figs were also a symbol of fertility.

CHAPTER THREE

To be or not to be

I never tracked my period; I went on instinct, letting my body tell me when it was coming. I realised I hadn't had that feeling for a long time. With fluttering nerves and excitement in my belly, I stopped to buy a pregnancy test at the pharmacy on my way home.

As I looked at the bank of options, I was reminded of the previous time I had chosen one. A torn condom had left me panic stricken. The pill was not an option for me. It left depression in its wake. We relied on condoms with no problems, until then. At the time, I didn't want a baby. I was fairly sure I would never want a baby. But if I did, I knew I would want the child to have a solid home, a place to root, not a rented apartment and uncertainty. We had recently moved to Ireland and were starting over. We needed to find our place in this new world, before considering the idea of bringing another person into it.

Back then, I cried at the horror of even considering ending a pregnancy, but I didn't want a baby. We contacted a family planning centre in Dublin. They offered me the morning after pill. I was worried senseless about what I would do if I was pregnant and the morning after pill didn't work. Abortion was illegal in Ireland. I called my friend Bev, in Oxford, to ask her about abortion in the UK. She promised to find out and get back to me. I could hear emotion in her voice, but she didn't judge. Sean didn't judge either. He didn't want to go the abortion route if it came to that, but he wasn't going to tell me what to do.

When the pregnancy test showed negative ten days later, I felt like I had broken through water for air. Unknown to me, Bev was just pregnant with her cherubic son that later sparked my maternal instinct in Oxford. She was devastated at the idea of an abortion, but she still sought out information and contacts for me. She told me that she kept thinking if I went through with it, she would forever think of the missing child who would have been the same age as her firstborn. I don't know what I would have done if the test was positive. Now as I looked at the pregnancy tests and wondered which one to choose, I was fizzy with anticipation. It was hard to believe I was the same person, just a few years later. We are all on a journey, constantly evolving and learning. Who I was back then, is so different to who I am now. My essence is the same, but my perspective has changed.

I read the blurb on the tests and bought the one with the highest accuracy rating. At home I waited for Sean to get back. When he finally arrived, I went upstairs to the bathroom. I was so excited it was easy to take the action required to activate the wand. Within minutes a pink '+' appeared in the indicator window. I felt an electric thrill, hugged my stomach, and yelled the news.

'Are you sure?' Sean shouted back.

'Certain,' I said, descending the stairs, brandishing the wand proudly.

'Wahoo!' exclaimed Sean and hugged me close.

I felt a deep well of delight. I hadn't expected to feel this euphoric. We stayed hugged together for a couple of minutes taking in the sensation.

'The Champagne has been waiting for the perfect occasion,' said Sean as he let me go. He rummaged into our small wine cellar and transferred the bottle to the freezer compartment of our fridge. 'That's our lives turned upside down.'

'I can't believe how happy I feel,' I said.

'Me too,' said Sean.

We did a quick calculation of when the baby would arrive.

'Perfect timing,' I said. 'Spring and summer for maternity leave. We couldn't have picked a better moment.'

'I'd better get a push on with studying, so I can have some down time. Birth in April, CFA exams in June. That's going to be fun.'

Sean popped the Champagne and poured a glass for himself, then looked at me, eyebrows raised.

'I'll have apple juice please, no wine for me,' I said in a saintly tone, emulating Penny.

He poured apple juice from a carton. It wasn't organic. We didn't buy much organic. Frank, a work colleague, and his wife Suzanne, had a smallholding an hour from

Dublin. They had started to sensitise us to why organic was important, so we bought some organic produce, but we hadn't fully grasped the importance of organic produce to our health.

Like Aideen and Barry, Frank and Suzanne had made me feel welcome when I arrived in Ireland. A school friend had worked with Suzanne in London. When she heard that I was going to Dublin she put us in touch via email. My second weekend in Dublin, Frank drove into the city to take me out to their place for the day. We had gin and tonics followed by a pot roast cooked on a two-ring gas burner, their only cooking facility during years of renovation. They didn't know me at all, but they went out of their way to make me feel part of their family that day, like I was at home.

Despite their diligent attempts at educating us, none of the wine in our cellar was organic. We didn't know grapes were one of the fruits with the highest pesticide residues, and hence one of the most important products to buy certified organic, along with apples, strawberries and nine others known as the 'dirty dozen'. We would learn the grisly details years later when we became organic farmers. At least we were gardening our patch outside organically.

We had survived for a year on Frank and Suzanne's two-ring gas cooker, serving us through the renovations, as it had them. We spent weekends doing DIY: painting walls and lifting carpets, their undersides garnished with old cigarettes and chip packets, while building up funds for the kitchen. Now, glasses in hand, we stood in our new galley kitchen, shiny glass, and stainless steel, with a range style cooker in the middle, Sean's delight. The pine floors were varnished and gleaming in the summer sun. We clinked glasses.

'*Slainté*!' said Sean using the Irish word to toast good health. 'To new life!'

'To new life!' I echoed, a sense of wonder at those words. Our eyes met. We knew it was momentous, but we had no idea what an adventure we were embarking on.

'I feel so excited,' I said.

'Me too,' replied Sean.

We basked in the feeling. Sean took a sip from his flute. 'This Champagne is rather good. Perfect for the occasion. Sorry you can't join me.'

'Don't be sorry. I don't even feel like drinking wine.'

The apple juice was making me feel slightly nauseous so there was no way I wanted Champagne. I gave the juice to Sean and took a glass of water instead.

A few days before, we met Aideen and Barry at a gastropub for dinner. Since I was the driver, I restricted myself to one glass of wine. The next day I felt like I had been kicked in the head. It was way worse than it should have been. Usually, a glass or two would have no bad effect. My unknown pregnancy had multiplied the hangover. My body was telling me to quit.

As Sean and I chatted about the new life inside me and how it would change our lives, I took a microwave dinner out of the freezer, removed the cardboard sleeve, and punched the plastic top. It was a regular practice for us mid-week, when we thought we didn't have enough time to prepare food. It was easy. Too easy. The ingredients list was packed with E numbers. I didn't think about it at the time. It was tasty and fast. I didn't think of the potential consequences of pesticides or plastic.

I went through my days walking on air, my soul filled with exhilaration and expectation. Even the mundane act of driving to work felt different. There was something going on inside me that charged the environment with special energy. I couldn't eat garlic, usually a favourite, and I couldn't face coffee. I gave up my dawn cappuccino on Baggot Street without regret. Even the smell of those things made me want to throw up. Strong tea, another favourite, didn't taste the same, but at least it didn't send me running for the nearest washroom.

Our world began to change in other ways. Instead of planning the next DIY project we read up about babies. I began to feel a little scared. I had never considered the danger of childbirth, but despite great advances, it remained a messy, and potentially perilous, affair.

When Penny and Andrew's beautiful daughter was born, we visited them in hospital. They were proud and delighted but Penny had had traumatic birth experience. Her long and painful labour ended in a caesarean. Until the surgery, her labouring was in a large open ward with no privacy, and she had no coaching from an experienced midwife. After the birth, Penny was keen to breastfeed but there was no-one to help her. With the pain of the caesarean, and the lack of support, she gave up. Entering motherhood was no easy ride. But it was too late for me.

I needed to educate myself. My friend Aideen, a volunteer breastfeeding counsellor and mother of two would be a good sounding board. Aideen and Barry were like family to us. After taking me under their wing when I arrived in Ireland, they had become an important part of our lives.

I stopped at their bungalow in Monkstown to share the news. Aideen danced around the room and gave me a hug. She made me a cup of herbal tea and sat down, notepad in hand. Aideen ran leadership development and management training in a large technology multinational, she knew how to bring people up to speed. With her, I would move swiftly from 'clueless' to 'clued-up'.

'Have you thought about where you want to have the baby?' asked Aideen.

'I haven't a clue,' I replied.

'Well, let's have a think. You have lots of options,' she said. 'You could go to a private hospital, or to a public one, like the Gurney, or Holles Street.'

Holles Street was the National Maternity Hospital, colloquially known by the name of the street outside.

'My friend Penny had a bad experience at the Gurney,' I said.

'And with where you work, Holles Street makes sense. So that's probably that decision made,' said Aideen. 'Next question, do you want a consultant obstetrician? Or do you want to go the public route, where it's mostly midwives, rather than a doctor?'

I lifted my eyebrows and pulled a 'no idea' face. Aideen caught my drift.

'Consultants are expensive, but they give you a sense of security especially for a first baby. They offer extra expertise that may not be necessary if everything goes smoothly. Thinking about it, if things don't go smoothly, you'll see a specialist anyway, but you won't be able to choose who.'

'So, a consultant is a specialist obstetrician?' I asked.

'Exactly. And if you want a consultant in Holles Street, these are the ones you could consider,' said Aideen, writing names on the notepad as she spoke.

'How do I decide?' I asked.

'Phone them and see. You'll know based on a few calls. Another good option in Holles Street is the Domino Programme. It's a special unit suited to people wanting a natural birth. They started small but have been so successful that they've extended to Killiney, lucky for you. With them you'll see midwives not doctors. They have a great reputation. If you like the sound of that, visit them to see if it's for you.'

'But, for security, a consultant makes sense?' I asked.

'Not necessarily. Like I said, there's always a specialist available if something goes wrong. Even if you go with a consultant, when you deliver, they could be down in Cork for holidays or on a weekend away, so you might not have the one you got to know in the run-up. In a crisis, like if you need a caesarean, a specialist consultant will be there to do it, no matter which route you take.'

We chatted for a while longer. As I prepared to leave, Aideen gave me another hug.

'I am so excited for you,' she said.

'Thanks Aideen. Me too. And a little scared.'

'Everything will be great. I'm here if you need advice. I'll get some books ready for you for next time you stop by.'

The following day I called the three consultant obstetricians Aideen had noted. Their prices made me hyper-ventilate, but more than the cost, the lack of love in their harassed secretaries' voices made me want to run a mile. When I entered the tiny room reserved for the Domino programme in Holles Street hospital,

I felt instantly accepted. The two midwives were warm and welcoming. On the wall were photographs of the nine nurses that ran the scheme with their names. They were the people who would take care of me through the pregnancy, and I would meet them all during my appointments over the coming months so I would know the person who delivered my baby. Most people had their baby attended by a midwife they had never met. It didn't seem right to be assisted by a stranger at one of the most intimate events in your life.

In the tiny, unpretentious space, I felt a real sense of care, a love for their work. It was the place for me. A couple of doors down from Holles Street, the classic Dublin door to my office, bold blue adorned with a large brass knocker, felt solid, as did my choice. A key part of my journey to motherhood was taken care of. The Domino programme was perfect. Life could not have offered me a better location to be pregnant.

A few days later, soon after getting home from work, I started bleeding. It felt like a period, but I knew I wasn't supposed to have those in pregnancy. I ran upstairs to the bathroom and saw it was worse than a period. As I looked at the blood pouring out of me, deep sobs instinctively rose. Once the blood slowed, I grabbed a towel, padded it around me like a nappy, then stared into the bowl, to see if there were signs of a tiny human. I only saw blood. Feeling faint with fear, I gripped the towel under me, and went downstairs to call the midwife hotline.

'How bad is the bleeding?' asked the midwife.

'It was like a very heavy period,' I said. 'Now it's slowed.'

'Is there someone who can bring you in?'

'No, but my husband should be home in about an hour,' I replied.

'If you're still bleeding when he gets home, come in straight away. If not, come in tomorrow and we'll organise a scan to check that everything's okay. Don't worry, sometimes this happens and it's nothing.'

I hung up, lay back on the sofa seeing stars and reflected on the word "sometimes". I called Sean but his mobile was off. I hoped it meant he was on his way. I was still there when I heard his key in the lock.

'Help,' I called. He crashed through the door, looking like a tall black insect in his cycling gear and goggles. His face told me he had listened to my message.

'I need a clean towel so we can see if it's stopped,' I said. 'It feels like it has.'

He ran upstairs to the airing cupboard, and returned, towel in hand. I exchanged it. The new towel stayed white. The bleeding had stopped. Sean grilled me about what the midwife had said. Then he made dinner quietly and I stayed on the sofa until he called me for a phone call from my grandmother Gigi.

'Hello, darling Caro,' said her familiar voice far away down a long line from the other end of the world, 'Congratulations.'

Tears started to flow down my cheeks. Feelings of love, hope, and fear, swirled inside me as her voice took me deep into my memory. Gigi lived in an old stone house in Matatiele, a small town in South Africa, on the southern border of the mountain kingdom of Lesotho. She was calling from that house where she grew up, and where my mother grew up, a place embedded in our family history.

As I listened to her voice, my mind reeled back to arriving there after my grandfather had died. It was a release for him; he had been in a battle with cancer for a long time. The remaining household looked haggard, beaten up by death passing through. My mum, my aunt, and two great aunts had been there to help Gigi in the last few weeks. There was a complicity between them, a special closeness, the day we arrived, a day after the funeral.

Sean and I were on our way to a cottage at my uncle's trading store at *Sehlabathebe*, the Place of Shields, in Lesotho, for a week of holidays. We thought we had a few days to share with Gigi, my mum, and my aunts, before leaving, but a crisis at the store meant our lift had to leave the following morning. The last-minute departure took everyone's minds off the sadness. Gigi threw herself into preparing food for us to take. The evening flew by in a dense exchange of cooking, chatting, and packing. Sean fit like a glove, participating in the preparation, and talking with everyone, like he had known them forever. It was the first time he met Gigi and my mum's extended family. The next morning, we said farewell to the tight core of my mum's tribe, sad to leave, but excited about our trip.

The route up to *Sehlabathebe* was more ravine than road, stark rocks, and mountain relief. Our wine for the holiday, a box red called Tassenberg, 'Tassies' for short, a student tradition, was tied on the back with our luggage, and supplies for the trading store. It was in full sun, and like us, well shaken, by the time my cousin dropped us at the rustic, sparsely furnished, cottage.

The habitation was basic but the nature that surrounded it was majestic. Mountains soared; giants in a circle around us. On the hook of the river, a cluster of huts spluttered smoke, sound, and movement. Late afternoon we walked down. In a natural pool, where the water slowed, I swam, and Sean watched. Local kids joined me and entertained us with antics. They jumped and dove, thrilled to have an audience.

It could have been any day of the week; anything could have happened in the outside world, and we wouldn't have known. There were no phones, televisions, or mobile signals, just a CB radio in the trading store, for emergencies.

In the evening, the mountains shrouded themselves in white cloaks. At 10 p.m., the hum of the generator stopped, and silence filled the deep starry night. Inside, flickering lights became flickering candles. A bark from a dog shot the silence of the studded sky. We sat on the sofa reading, our feet touching. I felt so happy and in love. I looked up and our eyes met, the sensation electric.

The next morning, the sunrise fingered across the mountains, like a great golden hand gently caressing them awake. In the valley, smoke poured out of a drum into the cool dawn air. We hiked all day and skinny dipped in a tarn, a lake, high in the mountains, the scene like a Tolkien film set. Sean was not the skinny-dipping type but given the remoteness, he succumbed. I swam into the middle, feeling as bright as the crystal-clear water. Sean joined me.

We floated on our backs, feeling freedom as broad as the blue sky above us.

'Enough for me, I'm heading back,' said Sean, a few minutes later.

I stayed where I was. The water felt so pure. I was starting to feel cold, but it was too good to leave. As Sean reached our neat pile of clothes, we heard the thrumming of hooves. Sean quickly pulled on his jeans as a herd of ponies and their Basuto carer galloped up to the lake. They tarried at the water, while I shivered in the middle, knees clutched to my chest, protecting my nakedness. The herdsman smiled, waved, and moved his ponies on. Relieved, I swam back and shook myself off. With clothes on and a good pace, I soon warmed up. That evening, the stars sparkled like there was a diamond cutter working overhead. The mountains surrounded us like a protective crown.

Back in Matatiele, after the trip, Gigi's figs were ripe, and bunches of mellow purple grapes hung from vines that covered the wooden arches over the dusty driveway. Claret roses planted by Gigi's mother gave off waves of heady scent. The grapes smelt like heaven and my taste buds soared with their burst of sweetness in my mouth.

Gigi looked lost and in shock. Her sisters and daughters had returned to their lives. She was alone and fifty-five years of uneasy marriage still made for a difficult adjustment to widowhood. Despite their rough partnership, my mum said that in their last few weeks together she had seen a tenderness between Gigi and my Grandad, that she hadn't seen before. There is power, instinct, and an animal quality to love, that we often forget in our focus on romance.

I saw in Gigi more than the loss of her husband, it was like she was allowing herself to feel, to express her emotions. She had always been the tough one, the one keeping the boat afloat, never free to feel in total abandon. She was the one that didn't need support, who, at eighty, still played bowls and climbed ladders to paint the house.

She reached out to hug me, speaking quietly of her grief. I had never seen Gigi emotional like that. She had carried the responsibility for her family as good as alone for the decades my Grandad succumbed to alcoholism. I hugged her and spoke words of compassion and love. I felt a light inside, a flame lit by the act of comforting her.

Sean, Gigi, and I spent that evening sharing memories and stories. She seemed fortified by our presence and the opportunity to talk. When we left the next morning, I was surprised by the strength of her eighty-year-old grip. We squeezed each other's hands through the car window. I looked into her eyes and tears welled up. We let go and Sean took off. At the garden gate I looked back, and we waved like fanatics, eyes unfocused through saltwater. Sean turned the corner, and I cried like I had lost her. It was the last time I visited that house.

Now her voice was far away, coming down a long cable under the sea, wishing us well with our baby on the way, the baby that may have died this evening. I felt the potential loss and swallowed hard to stop myself from sobbing. We read that it was best to keep the news to yourself for the first three months, in case something happened. Now I understood why. We had told our closest family, and a few select people like Aideen and Barry, but kept it relatively quiet. I tried to sound upbeat and didn't say a word about the bleed. I didn't want Gigi worried. She was a toughie, but she was nearly ninety.

I hung up. My voice had been stable, not giving anything away, but a pile of tissues beside me bore witness to tears that had rained down through the call. Sean came and sat with me on the sofa. He hugged me tenderly.

'Hang in there Caro. We'll find out tomorrow. There's no point in worrying about it. What will be will be.'

'I know Sean. I know that logically you're right, but I can't help it.'

I leaned into him, his strong arms surrounded me, giving me a sense of security, helping me calm down. What would be, would be. Tomorrow would tell.

Chapter Four

Yoga for anxiety

The following day, the doctor's room was as grey as my mood. Lying on the examination table, I lifted my shirt and the obstetrician rubbed gel onto my stomach. I closed my eyes briefly in prayer. When I opened them, he picked up the scanner and pressed it into my stomach sweeping this way and that. This way, that way. That way, this way. Up and down, round and round. My angst rose with each sweep. I tried to divine the news, but he was poker faced. He kept sweeping, impervious to my rising panic. At last, he stopped and pointed at the screen.

'There it is. The foetus looks fine. The heartbeat is strong.'

I felt the grey mood lift and a buzz of happiness take its place. He pushed a little harder, and took a screen shot from one angle, then another. According to his calculations, it was seven weeks since conception. In his photos I could see a perfectly formed being. I felt awed, excited, joyful, like dancing and singing with delight. Seeing this tiny person, I also felt shocked that I had considered the idea of an abortion a few years before.

'Could running have caused it?' I asked quietly.

'No. Running is not a reason for a bleed,' he said, wiping his scanner.

'So, what could have caused it?'

'We don't know. In the first trimester, the foetus attaching itself to the uterus can cause it. We call that 'implantation bleeding'.'

'What should I do to avoid it happening again?' I asked.

'Well, since we don't know what caused it, it's hard to say. There's nothing you can do about implantation bleeding. If it happens again, we'll have more cause for concern.'

In that moment, I was struck by how little we humans really knew about the workings of life, despite medical advances, and by how fragile life creation was.

'Should I continue running?' I asked.

'Take it easy for a week or two, stick to walking, see how things go, then start running again. Build it up slowly. Exercise in pregnancy is important. As you get closer to term, you'll probably want to stop running and do things like walking and yoga.'

With the scan prints nestled in my purse I walked on air down Merrion Road and up Baggot Street to Sean's office. Within seconds of asking for him at reception, I heard the clatter of his work shoes flying down the stairs. He burst into the entrance area. I gave a wide smile, and he hugged me. We crossed the Grand Canal to sit quietly on a bench and look in wonder at the scan as we held hands in the fresh autumn air. Orange, yellow, and gold leaves fluttered onto bright grass. The magnificent flaming tree silhouettes were doubled by their reflections on the water. The seasons continued, autumn on its path to winter, while inside me, a new life continued its miraculous path too.

'I have to get back,' said Sean, giving my hand a squeeze. 'Can you meet for lunch? Takeaways on the Canal to make the most of the good weather?'

He felt the same way I did. We needed to be together to celebrate this news, this tiny print that filled our hearts with joy.

'Good idea,' I said. 'See you at 12.30 at the usual place.'

❦

A few weeks later, a visit from my sister Foo promised to save me from takeaway lunches. She flew in from Canada to whisk me to Ballymaloe Country House Hotel for my birthday while Sean was in London for a CFA study weekend. Ballymaloe is one of the most highly regarded food destinations in Ireland. My pregnancy made me so nauseous I wondered how I would do it justice. When the cheese board arrived, I asked which were pasteurised. The waitress pointed to the most sterile looking option. No wine and no fabulous cheese for me.

Foo and her close friends didn't have kids. She couldn't understand how I had gone over to the other side, especially if it meant no fine wine and cheese. I explained my 'road to Damascus' and Foo looked at me like the alien that I was.

Back in Dublin my transformation continued. My stomach grew, progressing from a bulge to a distended rugby ball. It was a living thing that kicked and that I loved to stroke. It felt so weird but so good. Sitting on a yoga mat in a back garden studio in Monkstown, the size of my belly gave me a shock. I felt a jab of fear, of the unknown, of the process of birth. I was following the doctor's advice with regular walks and this new yoga class. The teacher went down into table-top pose.

'We breathe in as we lift our heads up and curve our bellybutton towards the floor, like a cow. And we breathe out and arch the spine towards the sky, dropping our heads down, like a cat. And in, and out. And in, and out. Keep that rhythm for another set of eight. Caro, the space between your hands should be about the width of your shoulders. And in and out.'

How could she see my hands? Did she have eyes in the sides of her chest? Whatever about her eyes, she had an incredible body, lithe and muscular, the essence of supple. Her movements and voice were calm and peaceful.

'Before continuing our movement, I'm going to lead you in a short loving kindness meditation. This is a simple, powerful way to cultivate positive thoughts for you, your baby, those around you, and the wider world. It's unconditional well-wishing, open-hearted kindness, to ourselves, and others. It helps to ground, and reconnect us, in difficult times. We tend to be hard on ourselves, to judge ourselves harshly. To be kind to your baby, you need to start by being kind to yourself.'

I felt like she was talking directly to me. I was pushing myself to keep up the same cadence of work and exercise as I had before. I needed to chill.

'Find your way into a comfortable seat that works best for you. Developing a practice of loving kindness, and compassionate self-acceptance, will help you meet the challenges of pregnancy and birth. We'll start with blessing ourselves, then our baby, then the wider world. Repeat after me. 'May I be filled with loving kindness.''

'May I be healthy.'

'May I be happy.'

We repeated each of her mantras. From there we repeated them for our babies.

'May you be filled with loving kindness.'

Then we passed the same messages onto the wider world. There was a sense of wellness in the process of following her chant. Part of me rejected it, found it too new age, but I was surprised by the feeling of peace it provided. She smoothly transitioned from the meditation into active yoga poses.

As she moved, she explained how yoga had helped her birth four children at home with *no anaesthetic.* The idea of achieving this mammoth feat with no pain relief made me feel dizzy, but her brief description also perversely made me want it. I liked the sound of walking around and continuing life as normal, minutes after giving birth. Natural birth became my mantra.

Aideen's books recommended squatting, squatting, and more squatting, as preparation for a natural birth. I read books while squatting, my feet parked out like a duck, toes just visible over my belly. I practised the poses recommended by my Wonder Woman yoga teacher. I put almond oil around the all-important exit and gently stretched it with my fingers as instructed. My body was on fire, hormones raging. They made me extremely amorous, but Sean didn't want to risk hurting the baby. I assured him there was no risk. I stocked up on the natural birth aids recommended by the midwives, relaxing oils,

TENS machine and a yoga ball. I practised my breathing exercises.

Every spare moment I gardened. There was something satisfying about it, seeing seemingly lifeless seeds sprout into small plants, then watching them grow. Our greenhouse, a glorified set of shelves wrapped in clear plastic, was packed with seed trays. With the damp weather in Ireland, our biggest enemies were snails and slugs. When the expensive Hosta disappeared overnight and a web of damning silver trails gave the thieves away, I declared war. Sean started a midnight patrol, catching them at their most active. We collected thousands, dropping them into heavily salted water for quick death. We left dead ones out, to send a message, but they kept coming. They knew a good organic garden. On clear nights, the sky full of stars and the sound of the sea, combined to fill us with awe, as we ranged across the garden making war on gastropods.

At work I tried to be one of those kick-ass mothers-to-be that kept going at the same pace as before they were pregnant. As co-founder of a consulting and early-stage venture capital firm, responsible for lead generation and marketing, I needed to be on the ball. My colleagues were mostly men, and all, save one, childfree. I felt alien to them, and to myself. I reminded myself of the loving kindness message from my yoga teacher. Who was the new emotional being that had taken over my body?

I walked into town to meet my friend Brigid at the National Gallery Café. She was expecting her second baby within days of mine. A cold wind froze my exposed ears and ruffled my short cut as I navigated from Lower Mount Street along Merrion Square, past the now familiar Holles Street Hospital, and onto Clare Street. In the distance, trees in Trinity College were stark and leafless against grey buildings and sky.

Near the entrance to the National Gallery two women, one of them pushing a buggy, were having an animated conversation, laughing and chatting. The baby's hat fell onto the sidewalk. The mum stopped to pick it up and popped it back into the buggy. A couple of seconds later, I saw the baby reach for it, and drop it out. They stopped and laughed exuberantly, as mum bent to pick it up again.

'Just like his dad,' she said. 'Anything to get my attention.'

Inside, the heat was a welcome contrast to outside. I took my coat and scarf off and hung them on the back of a chair. Brigid waved, bright colours swirling. We hugged. I told her what I had just seen.

'I can't believe how smart that baby was. He was jealous that his mom was chatting to her friend instead of giving her full attention to him. He knew exactly how to fix it with the hat trick. Incredible.'

'What can I say. They're little humans. They're smart. Perhaps more emotionally tuned in than we are, and definitely more instinctively tuned in,' said Brigid.

'I feel daunted Brig. I'm scared. What if I'm not up to being a mother? I feel like that baby just showed me how little I know.'

'It's the most amazing adventure, Caro. I know the heartburn and backache isn't great craic. Neither is needing to pee every five seconds. But look what you get. An amazing, beautiful baby.'

I laughed in complicity.

'Then once they're a toddler, you'll get to watch Barney a million times. You'll have just mopped the floor and they'll empty the pot of yoghurt onto it. Ha ha. But when they hug you, OMG. It makes everything worthwhile.'

'I can't wait,' I said, laughing. It was great to have a friend that was on the same track as me, but with experience.

The countdown of the last eight weeks started. Sean and I attended prenatal classes at Holles Street. How unbelievable it was, that a baby the size of my distended stomach would come out of my lower passage, hit home. I undertook the squatting and almond oil stretching even more diligently. I wondered if I would have been quite so keen that sunny spring day in our back garden if I had fully appreciated the 'baby getting out' part. The indignity of the process slammed home too. I learned that the pressure of birth meant that you would probably shit yourself. Just hearing about the pain, I was already shitting myself.

Something started growing on the left labia of my vagina. I contorted myself to view it with a handheld mirror and was filled with horror as I self-diagnosed a vaginal wart. The internet revealed that it was a dangerous little fecker that could infect the baby. I enlisted my husband to check it. The romance of the passage was totally blown, it had become a utility, a transport tunnel that needed to be cleared of dangerous material, and regularly stretched, unfortunately not in the way that I enjoyed. Sean could see the growth, but wisely, wouldn't diagnose. He recommended calling the midwives.

The midwives calmly booked me in for a check-up that day covering up their worry with measured tones. Filled with stress but also feeling the urge to laugh I climbed onto the examination bed and put my feet into the stirrups.

Sticking my feet into gynae stirrups gave me the jitters. I had never taken to it.

I tried some visualisation to ease my anxiety. Stirrups equals horse riding. I loved horse riding growing up. I imagined galloping through fields above the Cliffs of Moher on a gorgeous bay thoroughbred, hair flying, like on one of the Guinness ads. In the prenatal classes they taught us to visualise peaceful places to control the pain. This exciting adrenalin filled place seemed fitting to my agitated mind. My steed and I were leaping a stream when the intern obstetrician interrupted me.

'Hmm, yes, that's a vaginal wart, all right,' she said, peering into my most intimate part. 'I think there's another one over there too. I'll book you in to see a specialist gynaecologist to have them removed pronto.'

I absorbed the news with a racing heart and unhooked my feet from the stirrups. I felt responsible for putting my baby in danger. For the week between the assessment and the appointment I felt unclean. A vaginal wart was something I associated with promiscuity. I wondered how I had contracted it. Sean and I had been monogamous for more than a decade. I thought back through my beaux and wondered who could have passed this horrible blight to me. Had I infected Sean? I forced him to do a thorough check of the vital area. He assured me all was well. At least he didn't have to contort himself with a mirror.

At work it was hard to stay focused. I felt like a double agent. Half my mind on the meeting, half of it gnawing on my now compromised transport tunnel. When I wasn't at work, I gardened to find peace as I waited for the 'pronto' appointment. Weeding, digging, clearing leaves to make leaf mould, weeding, digging, and then more weeding.

At last, the hour arrived. I entered the doctor's office feeling more nervous than I usually did when I had to bare my vagina to someone I had never met. I tried the horse-riding visualisation again but failed. The gynaecologist investigated my private parts with a large magnifying glass.

'That's not a vaginal wart!' he exclaimed. 'Who said it was?'

I told him.

'Inexperienced interns,' he muttered under his breath. 'It's a benign growth of skin. You have a tsunami of growth hormones surging through your body to grow your baby. Sometimes they make other things grow too. I'll remove it for your comfort but it's nothing to worry about.'

The fecker was not a fecker but was swiftly removed anyway. I was so relieved I walked on air across the Grand Canal and called for Sean at his reception. We sat on the bench looking onto the water and I shared the news in hushed tones. With the crisis declared a non-crisis, I busied myself with the research and analysis for a report on the software industry, a key project I undertook each year for my business.

A few days later the buzzer next to the Georgian door of our office rang, and Sean's voice echoed through the intercom. I rose from my desk and lumbered to the top of the six flights that would take me to the ground floor. Taking those stairs several times a day, was a key part of my exercise regime. The size of my belly made going down a precarious affair. I gripped onto the balustrade and started my descent.

'Come on, come on, we'll be late!' said Sean when I finally reached the bottom. He grabbed my arm and marched me down Merrion Row to Holles Street reception.

Sean was super excited. We were about to experience the 38-week scan, the last one before the baby's predicted arrival at around 40 weeks. I felt excited too. The closer we got, the more 'real' the birth process became. I realised that midwives and friends didn't tell all, until you were almost there. They didn't want to alarm you, preferred to leave you in blissful ignorance.

We waited in the corridor at the door to the scanner's consulting room whispering quietly. At the first scan after the bleed, I felt so nervous, so worried. Now it was familiar. We were almost at term and I didn't feel worried at all.

The scanner ushered us in. She had a broad smile and an easy manner as she explained what she would do.

'Would you like to know the sex of the baby?' she asked.

'No. We prefer it to be a surprise,' I replied, looking to Sean to check he was still in agreement, and catching his hint of a nod. 'We read that it can be wrong and then your mindset is all messed up when the opposite arrives on the big day.'

She laughed.

'It's very unusual for it to be wrong, especially at this stage. But a lot of people still prefer to keep it a surprise.'

She began by slathering my tummy with gel, then pressed into it with the scanner, sliding back and forth through the slippery substance. She pointed to different parts of the being that had taken over my belly. The form was perfect, we could see everything, head, hands, feet, and I almost thought an expression of 'hey, stop invading my safe womb with your scan waves'. I looked up. Sean had a look of total adoration on his face. For me, this being kicked regularly and was omni-present. For Sean, the scan was a moment of meeting, of wonder.

When the scan was complete, she wiped the gel off my skin and talked through what to do in the next two weeks.

'It's important, especially if you want an active natural birth, to eat healthy, and stay fit. Lots of walking and gentle activity like yoga.'

Some days I didn't feel like walking, especially with my monster belly, but each time I did, I felt good. I knew I had to keep it up, now more than ever. My yoga class had finished so it was up to me to keep that up on my own now too.

'It could arrive early so be prepared,' she said, as a final bit of advice.

That night I had a nightmare about my baby falling off the edge of a walled pier and down, down, down into the dark sea. I dived in, but the baby sank faster than I could swim. I woke up in a cold sweat with the image of the top of my baby's head disappearing far below me into the deep ocean.

CHAPTER FIVE

The waiting game

My maternity leave started. I became a lady of leisure, filling my days with chatting with friends, reading and walking. Brigid, my friend who was expecting her second baby within days of mine, visited. We took a stroll along the raised path that led from our housing estate to Killiney beach. The sky was bright blue, the wind off the sea fresh.

Brigid was a can-do, no-nonsense woman; she played guitar like Neil Young and took to motherhood like she was born to it. Pippa, her first child, was around two years old, a red-haired beauty with an impish face. She gambolled next to us, as we rolled along with our great bellies. I wondered how Brigid coped with a toddler and a massive stomach; she looked blooming.

We paused and she hunted in the buggy for a packet of crisps, opened it, and gave it to Pippa. We continued walking, enjoying the bright sun, the rhythmic whoosh of the waves on the pebble stones, and the glittering sea.

'So, Caro, how are you?' asked Brig as Pippa stopped to look at a dandelion.

'I feel good, but I'm ready to have this baby now.'

'Enjoy it! It's the only peace you'll have for a long time.' Pippa dropped half her packet of crisps onto the concrete path. 'See?' said Brigid and laughed.

'Pick them up and eat them,' she said to Pippa.

'On this path, where people walk their dogs?' I asked.

'It's great for their immunity,' replied Brigid. 'God, at this age, if she didn't eat things she dropped on the floor, she'd hardly eat anything.'

Pippa picked up the bigger crisps and ate them.

'They drop things, they fall over,' said Brigid.

On cue, Pippa fell over. My heart rate took off like a bullet train. Brigid showed no sign of panic.

'What can I say?' she said and raised her eyebrows.

Pippa got back up without a murmur and carried on as if nothing had happened. I tried to calm my racing heart.

It was good to be with my friend in the cold air tinged with seaweed and salt. At the end of the walkway, we turned and made our way back. Pippa fell intermittently and picked herself up, and dropped crisps and then ate them.

At home, Pippa appeared as healthy as ever, no ill effects from the crisps or the falls. Brigid looked like she had been at a spa for the morning, and I felt like I needed one. I was finished, totally exhausted by the intensity of watching a toddler for barely an hour. What had I done?

Brigid lived on the other side of Dublin so meeting when I was at work was easier than now that I was on maternity leave. I didn't have a neighbourhood friend that had young children or was about to have them. Fortunately, that was about to change. A couple of days later, under a bright sky, the sea breeze stiff and fresh as newly starched sheets, I met Annetta. She was walking with her toddler and baby. We connected at the entrance to the path to the sea and chatted all the way to the beach. Annetta was a scientist working as a part time researcher at University College Dublin (UCD), and her house was on the path I took to the sea. She was an expat like me. Her Irish husband worked in tech like I did. We shared common ground and enjoyed each other's company.

From then on, Annetta and I regularly walked the route that I had walked with Brigid. She took her boys down to play on the beach almost every day. We compared our respective cultures with our adopted Ireland, gossiped about our husbands and discussed the challenges of raising a family as a working mum. It felt good to have a new friend who knew the ropes of motherhood.

If I hadn't met Annetta by the sea that day, I would have gone days without speaking to anyone except Sean as I waited for my baby to arrive. It was a strange world for me compared to my business life packed with intense human interaction, meetings, workshops, interviews, and *craic*. My work colleagues guaranteed a good dose of Irish banter with the working day.

My mum flew in, set to stay with us for four weeks. Her arrival was carefully planned, pitched a week before the due date. The time was allocated, the team was in place, the equipment was lined up. We were ready. There was a record stretch of sunny days. Mum and I took long walks on the beach. We gardened, we made and ate good food.

My parents lived in Canada, so we rarely saw them. Being together, just the two of us, made me aware of what we missed, living on different continents.

The first few days were a magical holiday. As days extended to weeks, the holiday feeling was marred by the return of the nightmare of my baby falling into the water. Each time I dreamt it, I woke filled with dread, and a feeling of desperate impotence. It kept coming back. The discomfort of a large belly and pressure on my bladder disrupted my sleep. The nightmare made it worse. I wondered what it meant. Was it a premonition? But our scan was perfect. My baby was moving normally. I put the recurring nightmare down to first birth nerves and told myself to get a grip.

The due date came and went. The scanner's warning turned out to be wrong, there was no early birth for me. Mum's precious time, meant to be spent helping me with the baby, turned into waiting time. I felt like we were treading water.

One of my work projects, the annual report on the state of the software industry, launched a week after my due date. Given there was no sign of labour, my mum and I attended the industry event to present the findings. I proudly introduced her, beautifully turned out in a chic spring outfit, while I lumbered about in a shapeless maternity tent. I was secretly delighted the baby had waited long enough for me to be there. Seeing my work colleagues and the who's who of the Irish software industry made me forget the waiting.

A couple of days later as I cleaned up after dinner, I felt a gush of hot water between my legs. I stared in horror at the pool forming on the floor.

'Help Mam,' I shouted.

'Don't worry, Toots. You're not incontinent. Your waters have broken,' said Mam appearing at the door. 'That should hurry things up.'

My mum and dad called me 'Toots'. I called mum 'Mam', a shortening of the French *Maman*, and perfect for life in Ireland where you didn't have a mum, you had a mam, or a mammy.

Mam was agitated with the waiting. She didn't say it directly, but her comment underlined it. Mam had specialised as a midwife when she trained as a nurse forty years before. She kept assuring us that it was so long ago, she had forgotten everything. It seemed true. When we asked her about the conditions of my birth, she remembered nothing. Perhaps the amnesia was to block the memory of extreme pain.

Sean turned to the internet for wisdom on breaking of the waters. He read the screen as he dialled the midwives. I climbed the stairs to wash and change into dry clothes leaving Mam to clean the kitchen floor. The midwife asked a few questions then advised.

'Don't panic. Your wife can shower but not bath. Stay tuned for contractions and when you come in for your planned appointment tomorrow bring an overnight bag in case.'

Sean yelled up 'no bathing'. I turned off the taps, made a mental note to cross 'calming bath with essential oils' off my carefully constructed 'contraction pain management' plan and got into the shower. In the morning, as we took the familiar Rock Road to the hospital, there was no sign of a contraction, not even a teensy-weensy one.

'I don't want an induced birth,' I said, as I watched the Blackrock shopping centre pass, followed by a picturesque stretch of sea.

'Well, what can we do to hurry it up?' asked Sean.

'The midwives recommend sex.'

'I think it's too late for that, we're hardly going to do it in Merrion Square,' he said.

I pictured a lovely bit of grass in a relatively private section of the garden and considered arguing the point but decided better of it.

'Maybe they'll send us home again,' I said.

'Your mum's in the house,' said Sean, dashing my hopes.

From glimpses of calm sea, we turned to the tree-lined avenues of Donnybrook, then plunged into the city with its low-rise buildings, pubs, and Georgian buildings of Merrion Square.

Aromas of damp under-brush and forest floor from the light woodland in Merrion Square mingled with the carbon dioxide of a multitude of cars that circled looking for parking spaces. The sun caught the blue clock at the top of the maternity hospital building. The piercing pitch of a siren broke the peaceful hum of cars and people. I felt extra alert, senses acute. Sean gripped my arm protectively and we crossed the road.

We signed in at hospital reception then took the stairs up to the Domino Programme's waiting area, a makeshift row of chairs against the wall of the corridor outside their consulting room. Lara opened the door and ushered us in, asking questions about the breaking of the waters, as she installed me on the trolley bed that served as their diagnostic table. She checked me over, felt my belly, checked my blood pressure, and then did the finger check.

I found having someone other than my lover, or myself, insert a body part into my vagina, disconcerting.

'All's well,' she declared. 'We can wait one more day. If nothing's happening by then we'll have to induce you.'

'I don't want induction,' I said. 'I read induction means a more intense and painful labour, that it reduces the likelihood of a natural birth.'

'That's true,' said Lara. 'But the risk of infection increases once the waters have broken. We can wait 24 to 48 hours if all's well, but after that, we recommend induction, for the baby's health and yours.'

That night, light contractions started around 3 a.m., and I was delighted by the pain. The midwife hotline recommended paracetamol and said I must come in the following morning regardless of the progress of the contractions. We couldn't wait until the contractions were advanced, like we would have if the waters hadn't broken.

Driving in a few hours later I felt the odd twinge, but it was far from the panicked rush in the final throes of labour I had pictured. The sun was shining, spring was in the air. We were tranquil. Sean circled round Merrion Square and found a parking space. He put the maximum fee into the meter and left a note requesting that, given the circumstances, they not clamp the car if the meter had run out.

Inside the midwife on duty gave me the once-over.

'You're advanced enough that we don't need the induction gel, just the oxytocin drip,' she concluded as she removed her gloves. She picked up the phone to call the Domino birthing room. It had just become vacant. She sent us up.

CHAPTER SIX

Induction for speed

S ounds of labouring and intermittent screams from the birthing wards came down the passage to greet us. I said, 'Thank you, God' as we checked into the Domino room with en-suite bathroom. I had to face the drip but at least we had privacy. I had been warned there was only one room. If the Domino programme had another birth going on, I would have had to go to a standard birthing ward.

'Settle yourself on the bed so that I can put the drip in, there's a pet,' said Ann, a midwife I had met very briefly on my visits in the run-up. 'You'll hardly feel a thing; just a little nick.'

She was right, I hardly felt a thing. Sean put my bag on the floor and rummaged through it for the TENS machine and the calming oils. He put them on the side table, and we chatted about this and that.

As I sat on the bed, I wondered what all the fuss about birth pain was. Perhaps it wasn't as bad as everyone had led me to believe. Perhaps I was tough and didn't feel the pain like everyone else. An hour later my notions were rudely corrected. The induction fluid took effect and the contractions hit with fury. From barely feeling them an hour before, they came like an unstoppable army, wave, upon wave, of pain.

Gone was the tranquillity. Gone were my ideas of managing pain. The TENS machine and calming oils sat ignored on the table. The pain was so aggressive I knew they were futile, and anyway, with the pain of the contractions, I couldn't bear having anything touch me. Sean coached me on breathing. I pushed the IV pole round the room, keeping moving to cope, ignoring him, and bending over intermittently to push the pain out with a loud 'aarrgghhh' as my gut contracted. My entire being focused on second-to-second survival, on getting through a contraction, and having a moment to breathe before the next one.

Through my haze of agony, I saw the birth team huddle in discussion. I continued to circle like a crazed filly, the drip's metal stand gripped in a white-knuckled hand. Ann pulled out of the huddle.

'We need you to lie on the bed,' she said, backing away as I curved back around.

'Why?' I asked and continued moving, then stopped to lean on the wall as another contraction hit. 'Aaargghh.'

I started moving again.

'We need to check the heart rate,' said Ann, keeping up with me. 'We need to place wires on your stomach to monitor the contractions and the heartbeat of your baby.'

'Can I move around again after?' I asked.

'Probably. But we must do it, and we must do it now. Get up on the bed before another contraction hits.'

They wired me up. I was desperate to move. The pain was too much. I begged to get off. Ann unplugged me and let me have another few minutes of circling. Another huddle formed. I felt wild, like I would bolt if I wasn't attached to the drip and weighed down by my belly.

Ann approached me again.

'We need you back on the bed. We need to monitor the contractions. We also need to check the baby's oxygen levels,' she said. 'You must lie down. The doctor needs to take a blood sample from the baby.'

'Why?'

'The heart rate's changing with each contraction. We need to check that the baby's getting enough oxygen. We didn't do it until now because there weren't enough contractions to worry.'

I staggered to the bed, leaned on it, head down, as the pain of another contraction racked through me. Sean moved to help me.

'Don't touch me!' I yelled. My body was throbbing, a touch on the wrong spot would tip me over the edge.

I lay down like a big tummy pregnant woman cartoon, one hand holding my lower back and the other trying to ease my great bulk into the bed. Ann quickly stuck the monitor wires back onto my stomach and the doctor approached the bottom of the bed with gloved hands. A tidal wave contraction hit as he started to dig around inside my vagina.

'Aarghh!' I yelled and rolled sideways. He backed off. As soon as the tsunami passed, he came in to try again. And again. And again. After four failed attempts he took a break. A few minutes later he returned. This time he was successful.

Taking a blood sample from the baby meant scratching the baby's head. The baby didn't like it and neither did I, but the baby's oxygen level was okay. Relief flooded over me until another contraction hit and I rolled into a ball on my side. I tried to remember what I had learned about how to manage pain, but the build-up was too fast. I didn't have time to adjust to the rising contractions. They came in such quick succession I couldn't gather resistance and courage. I curled into a ball on the bed. The doctor approached to check the oxygen again.

The ball of pain that was my body drew back in horror. I couldn't take another failed oxygen test.

'We have to put a permanent oxygen probe on,' said Ann gently. 'It's too risky for the baby not to. We didn't do it until now because it means you won't be able to get up again.'

I groaned.

'We have to do it, Caro,' said Sean. 'It's for the baby.'

I screamed as another wave hit. As I came out of it sweating and swearing, Sean fixed me with a look that took control.

'Do what the doctor says. Now. While you have a gap in the contractions.'

I obeyed. Sean tried to help me again.

'Don't touch me!' I screamed, then moved to where the doctor needed me so he could attach the permanent oxygen monitor. Another contraction hit. As it subsided, he went in fast, sticking his hand up my vagina and attaching a tiny clamp to the baby's head on the first go.

Now I had the drip attached to my arm, multiple wires stuck to my stomach to monitor the contractions and the baby's heartbeat, and a wire coming out of my vagina. Movement on the bed was limited and walking was impossible. The contractions were galloping together in an almost constant stream of agony.

'Turn off the oxytocin!' I heard myself yelling.

'We can't,' said Ann firmly. 'We need labour to progress, given the changing heartbeat.'

'I can't take the pain anymore. I want it off!' I screamed. She checked my dilation.

'You're only two centimetres. We can't turn it off.' Her voice was calm, but firm, like she was talking to a toddler. 'Try some laughing gas.'

She passed me the gas mask and I took a deep drag. I waited in vain for a positive effect. The pain was as bad as ever.

'I want the drip off NOW! I want an epidural NOW!' I screamed. Another surge of pain gripped my body. I grabbed the gas again, then drew the mask away from my face.

'I want an epidural NOW!' I screamed. In case they had missed my point.

My natural birth mantra was forgotten. We were still a long way from the arrival of my baby. My cervix had to go from two to ten centimetres. Even in my pain-frenzied state I could calculate that we were only a fifth of the way. I could not imagine going through what I had endured another four times over. I would rather be dead. Another half hour of this hell, let alone several, was not possible.

It was not going to be a natural birth; the induction intervention had assured that. I had read horror stories of epidurals going wrong, but I was willing to do anything to turn off the agony. A huddle of midwives and interns formed at the end of my bed. They were joined by the professor of obstetrics. They debated my condition like I wasn't there.

I felt like an animal. Primeval screaming poured out of me with each contraction. The sound seemed like it was coming from someone else, but it was me. It was completely instinctive. My conscious brain wasn't managing it, my subconscious was. It was a release. I picked up snippets of their debate between screams.

Did I need a caesarean? If I did, would a general anaesthetic be required? Which meant I shouldn't have an epidural. Or was 'natural', that is, non-caesarean, still possible? In which case, the epidural was necessary to stop me disturbing the entire hospital, if not the whole of Merrion Square.

I had never considered a caesarean for my birth. I didn't want a medical event, but at that moment I would have done anything to shut out the pain. They decided natural, as in no caesarean, rather than no painkillers, was possible, and that I should be allowed to have an epidural. After what felt like hours, but must have been minutes, an anaesthetist arrived, syringe in hand. The needle looked long enough to go through my entire body not just into my spine. Usually, the sight of a small syringe made me pass out, but this time, I couldn't wait for him to plunge the hostile instrument into me.

I rolled onto my side exposing my vertebrae as he demanded. I had to stay totally still, difficult to do with the waves of pain, but he explained it was a matter of life, death, or permanent paralysis. Lara, the midwife who had taken over from Ann, helped to time the intervention in a gap between contractions. I kept still, and in seconds, was pain free. My outlook was transformed.

With no pain, I allowed myself to be pulled and prodded in any way they wished. My focus on surviving the agony was replaced by worry about my baby. Why were they doing all the oxygen checks? If there was a risk, why hadn't we gone to theatre for a caesarean?

Sean stepped out to update my mum. She started a chain of family and friends praying for a swift and safe delivery. The professor came back, felt around in my vagina, and announced I was dilated nine centimetres and would deliver within the hour. The oxygen level of the baby was still okay. I thanked God.

Within minutes the birth was imminent, and I was coached to push. Lara timed her instructions with contractions on the screen. With no feeling in my belly, it was a strange sensation, like watching myself on video rather than being there. I was surrounded by people: interns, midwives, the professor. It was about as far from my imagined natural birth as it could be, it was a medical event.

'I can see the head!' said Lara.

More pushes, no result.

'We need to make a small cut to allow the baby to come out,' said Lara. 'Is that okay?'

'Do whatever you need to do,' I said, waving nonchalantly, safe in my epidural protection.

An intern approached the end of the bed with large scissors, like the poultry shears in our kitchen drawer. There was a snip, and I felt a small sensation but no pain. Someone clamped a ventouse suction cup onto the baby's head and I felt a release, like I was emptying myself. A tiny being slithered out. My empty stomach, now a small bulge, lay before me. Beyond that, in the middle of the huddle of medical staff, Lara gripped our baby. After the marathon build up, the final part had gone so fast, I felt quite stunned.

'It's a girl!' said Lara. Someone cut the cord and whisked the baby to a table at the back of the room.

'What are they doing?' I asked, frustrated that I was immobile. The baby's head followed my voice amongst the chaos of her first moments in the world. She moved slowly like ET. I wondered why she wasn't crying. Years before I had read a myth that the doctor smacked the baby's bottom when they were born so they started crying and, hence, breathing.

'The paediatrician is checking the baby's vital statistics, the Agpar score,' said Lara.

Seconds later Lara placed our baby onto my stomach. Sean leaned over and looked at our girl, his face filled with adoration. I still felt in shock, awed by the experience, uncertain. But as I looked at the tiny face on my chest, a deep sense of wonder and love settled over me.

'She had the umbilical cord around her neck, that's why her heart rate changed with the contractions. That didn't make the birth any easier for her. Poor little dote,' said Lara, using an informal Irish term for someone considered adorable.

Our daughter's face was crumpled from the tough birth but to me, she looked quite perfect. Her movements were gentle like she was still swimming in the womb. She was quiet. Her little hand reached up and her eyes focused on my head where she could hear the familiar voice. I felt a connection to her, a love that went into my core. Sean put an arm around me and his other hand on her blanket. It felt like the three of us were enclosed in a cocoon, a protective circle, like nothing could touch us, secure as we were in the power of love that was in and around us at that moment. I began to understand Bev's words 'deepest love'.

Lara interrupted our devotion to pass our baby back to the paediatrician for a second check. She looked relieved as she handed our girl back to me.

'We'll get her feeding, shall we?' she said.

She helped me to get our baby latched on to my breast. The tiny girl sucked weakly and coughed up yellow froth. I looked questioningly at Lara. I had never done this before and had no idea what it was supposed to be like.

'She probably swallowed liquid during the drawn-out birth. She's tired out. Try again later, when she's had a chance to rest,' said Lara. 'Dara's taking over from me now. I'll pop in to see you tomorrow morning at the start of my day. Have a good rest. You deserve it. Congratulations to both of you.'

'Thank you, Lara, you were amazing,' I said.

Lara had been a perfect intermediary between us and the 'medical' team. She had fulfilled exactly what I expected when I chose the Domino programme. After she left, I stared at the tiny creature in my arms, not too sure what to do.

'We need a name for her,' I said.

Sean searched the duffel bag for the notebook with our list of baby names and my worthless 'pain management plan'. There were five girl and five boy names. With barely a discussion, we agreed she was Sophia. None of the other names matched her. She had already illustrated a peaceful and wise approach with her slow steady movements.

Dara took Sophia from me and prepared to bath her with help from Sean. I read that they don't wash babies after birth now as the natural oils are important to their delicate skin and help avoid eczema and other skin problems later in life.

The doctor that had snipped my vagina massaged my stomach to help the post birth contractions kick out the afterbirth. With its departure my stomach went a little flatter. She held up the bloody placenta. It was enormous, bigger than I expected, about the size of an empty leather rugby ball but thicker.

'Do you want it?' she asked.

I turned to Sean. He shook his head.

'We have to ask. Some people want to take it home. Some people bury it at the bottom of their garden. In some cultures, people eat it,' said the doctor.

'You sure you don't want to eat it?' I asked Sean.

He shook his head and pulled a face. We all laughed.

'Bury it at the bottom of the garden?'

He shook his head again.

'You sure? Could be good for the compost,' I said. I hated saying goodbye to things.

'No,' said Sean decisively. 'It would attract rats.'

I conceded and the intern disappeared with it. Sean knew I hated rats and that was one way to stop my hoarding nature in its tracks.

Now I felt useless, unable to participate in my half-paralysed state. I wanted to help with washing my daughter, who was loving her first bath, kicking about happily, but all I could do was lie in bed and watch. The epidural had been worth it though. The doctor returned from disposing of the placenta and approached the end of my bed again. The bottom of my bed felt like a train station, there had been so many people coming and going.

'I'm going to sew you up now,' she said, pulling up a swivel stool.

'Okay,' I said.

The large, curved, suturing needle looked like the one for leather work in my grandmother's sewing kit. I winced at the thought of what she was about to do. I was a medical wimp. The sight of blood made me faint. She took the first stitch and pulled the needle taught, almost to the height of her head. The black thread was decorated with tiny gobs of blood and flesh. I felt faintly nauseous but didn't pass out. She continued methodically. I felt the tug and pull but no pain. I didn't count the stitches, but it seemed like a lot.

'There. Almost as good as new,' she said proudly. 'When you go to the toilet, splash the wound with tea tree oil mixed with water. That'll help guard against infection.'

I nodded. The intern wished us well and left. My attention turned back to our daughter who Sean was dressing in a tiny Babygro. She looked so perfect.

We heard later that the one-minute Agpar score was 4/10 but the five-minute one was up to 8/10 so the paediatrician was satisfied and tagged the first bad score down to a lack of oxygen from the umbilical cord around her neck. Knowing that I understood Lara's look of relief after the second one.

Dara moved us down to a shared recovery ward, me in a wheelchair with Sophia in my arms, and Sean at our side. At the bedside Sean took Sophia from me and the nurses lifted me onto the bed. A metal cot stood beside it and on the other side, a dirty window looked onto a parking lot.

I tried to latch Sophia on again, but she spewed up more yellow mucus. I felt unsure. She seemed so delicate. I didn't know what to do.

'It's from swallowing amniotic fluid during the birth,' assured Dara, taking her from me and putting her in the cot.

Since the waters were long broken there couldn't have been much amniotic fluid left, but that didn't cross my exhausted mind. Dara recommended we get some rest. She introduced us to the night nurses, then left. Sean needed to get home too. It didn't feel right for the father to leave his precious family after such a momentous life event, but he had to, there was nowhere for him to sleep, and in my state, I couldn't go home.

Sean said goodnight and kissed me gently, then kissed Sophia's tiny forehead. It was hard to leave. I waved him goodbye and then pictured him walking into the cold night, back to the car on Merrion Square, and then along the Rock Road to home. I was in that reverie and feeling drowsy when the night nurse came in.

'Do you want Sophia at your side or next to us in the baby ward?' she asked.

'I think it's safer if she's next to you,' I said. 'What if she can't breathe in the night with all this mucus? I'm so tired and drugged up, I probably won't hear.'

'Yes, she's probably better next to us, so we can suction her if needed,' she said.

It felt wrong, but after little sleep in the previous 48 hours I knew it was the safest choice. By midnight the epidural began to wear off and I got up to try to check on

Sophia but saw stars and returned to bed. At dawn I woke again. This time I found Sophia. The little ward where she lay was stark and empty. She was alone, but it was two metres down the corridor from the nurses' office.

They had suctioned her a few times through the night and recommended I leave her to sleep. An hour later she woke. One of the nurses brought her through and we tried to get her latched on for a feed. She was spitting up so much yellow stuff that she couldn't. I was a medical dummy, but common sense told me this wasn't right.

'There's something wrong,' I said.

'It's just the mucus from the birth. We'll get the paediatrician to look in on his rounds later this morning,' said the nurse.

'Can't you do something faster than that?' I asked.

'We'll see what we can do. Relax and get some rest,' said the nurse.

I felt like saying 'Relax? Get some rest? For feck's sake!'

I told myself to trust the specialists. I accepted her authority despite my gut saying otherwise, and lay back on the bed, an eye on my precious baby. She looked paler than the night before. I had to do something. I got up to talk to the nurses again and got the same reaction. I went out to phone home. Sean had just woken up.

'There's something wrong,' I said. 'They keep saying that Sophia has swallowed a lot of amniotic fluid but she's still not feeding. She seems weaker this morning.'

'We'll get ready and come as soon as we can,' said Sean. 'Your mum wants to come in too, so she can meet Sophia and help us bring her home.'

Perhaps I was overreacting. After all, I didn't know what a newborn should look like. I hung up. Sophia appeared stiller and paler by the minute. I felt helpless. At last, the paediatrician, a tall, thin man with sandy hair and kind blue eyes, showed up.

'The nurses told me you were worried about the baby,' he said.

'She keeps spewing up yellow froth,' I said. 'She hasn't been able to feed.'

He checked Sophia's vital statistics.

'I don't think it's anything to worry about. We'll pump her stomach. That should do it. She'll be back within a half hour. It's fairly routine for a baby to swallow fluid in the birth,' he said, and picked Sophia up.

As his white coat disappeared through the ward doors, I felt a stab of adrenalin. I called Sean and asked him to come in straight away. He and Mam were preparing to leave.

I told myself to calm down and reached for the magazine stashed in my overnight bag. Perhaps the Doctor was right, a quick stomach pump and everything would be okay. I started to flick the pages. Half an hour passed. I was close to the end of the magazine and could feel tension rising inside me. As I put the magazine down, Sean and Mam arrived.

'Congratulations, Toots!' said Mam and gave me a warm hug.

Mam still thought everything was okay. With each minute past the promised half hour, I knew it wasn't.

Part 2: Life

'Healing is a matter of time, but it is sometimes also a matter of opportunity.'

Hippocrates

CHAPTER SEVEN

Transfer to a parallel universe

I t was twenty minutes past his estimate when the paediatrician came back without our baby.

'I'm afraid we have a problem,' he said.

Blood drained from my head, and I leaned back to steady myself on the bed. Everything was not okay. Stars bounced around in my vision of the doctor's talking head, his voice far away like a dream.

'Your daughter has oesophageal atresia. Her food pipe is a dead end and doesn't connect to her stomach. That's why she can't swallow.'

I felt like I had been punched in the stomach and gripped onto the bed to keep my balance. Sean's eyes connected with mine in shared anguish. Tears rushed down my face. Sean turned to the window to gain control of his. Without explanation, it was clear that this abnormality could be fatal. With no way of ingesting sustenance Sophia would die.

Sean wiped a sleeve over his tears then turned to face the doctor and said, 'Is there anything we can do?'

'We should be able to fix it,' said Dr Murphy.

I felt a shaft of hope through the shock.

He took a piece of paper and drew a diagram of what the dead-end oesophagus looked like, then explained the surgery that could be done, talking us through it, as he drew.

'So, as I said, usually it's possible to fix this problem, but it's complex, and it must be done by neonatal specialists,' he concluded.

'What do we need to do to make it happen?' I asked, going into project management mode.

'We've already started the process,' he said.

'How quickly can it be done?' I asked.

'How quickly will depend on availability of the theatre and the surgeon at Temple Street Children's University Hospital, where we plan to send her. You can come up and see her now, before she's transferred, then you can go home and wait to hear from Temple Street.'

What? Leave our newborn not knowing if we would see her alive again? Go home and wait? Sean and I exchanged a look of fear, then followed obediently.

The paediatrician led us out into a back corridor reserved for staff. Holles Street was an old hospital with polished red floors, and stairs, rather than lifts, in some parts. Mam, Sean, and I tracked behind him. As I climbed the stairs, I felt no pain, just a clear focus on the moment. The stitches and bruising of the night before were blocked out, forgotten. I wondered if I was in a bad dream and would wake up in a few minutes and find my daughter safe beside my hospital bed.

The Holles Street Intensive Care Unit (ICU) was filled with incubators and Sophia was tranquilly posed in one. She could have been a newborn model, she was so perfect, like a porcelain doll. The only give-away that anything was wrong, was the drip attached to her arm. She looked better than she had when she left me, dehydrated, fifteen hours since her cord was cut.

The paediatrician, Dr Murphy, showed us the X-rays, and re-explained the situation, and how it could be fixed.

'Can we go with her in the ambulance?' I asked.

'Unfortunately, no. The team at Temple Street need a few hours to do their checks and to confirm my diagnosis before you can see her again.'

We were firmly shown the door as Sophia had to be prepared to be transferred.

It was all too fast. I struggled to process what was happening. My brain raced ahead to when and in what circumstances we would see her again. I tried to rein it in to save myself. Back in the ward, seeing the other mums with their babies at their sides, I felt tears well up. I bit my teeth together and made my hands into fists against my stomach to focus on strength and swallow them back. This was not a place for crying and impinging the joy of the other mums.

Lara came up to see us, and to check that we understood the next steps. She said the Domino midwives would stay in touch but couldn't do any more at that point. I understood their position, but I had pictured them with us all the way, and right then, the message created a sense of abandonment. I gathered up my belongings and put them into my bag feeling lost, like I was missing something critical. My daughter.

Discharged from the maternity hospital, Sean drove us home in silence. We were all in shock. Instead of returning with our newborn, we were empty-handed, and desperately worried. At home, Mam became communications central telling family, friends, and neighbours, to save us from having to share the news. I knew I would break if I tried. Sean researched the condition on the Internet, and we became more frightened with each additional article.

Almost half of the children with this rare condition had other abnormalities, like heart or kidney malfunction. Until 1939, when the first successful operation of this type took place, all children with the condition died, so it was not a hereditary problem.

Since then, the success rate had slowly increased to almost 80 percent at that moment. There was a four in five chance Sophia would make it if the operation could be done. For the lucky ones that lived, there could be serious complications. Eventually Sean closed the browser, determined not to look at any more information. We wondered why we hadn't heard from the hospital and decided we would call after I had had a shower.

As I towelled myself dry, Dr Kapur called.

Sean put the phone on speaker, and I opened the bathroom door so I could hear.

'Our diagnosis concurs with Dr Murphy. We plan to go ahead with the surgery,' said Dr Kapur. 'I have to make you aware that all surgery has risks.'

He outlined what they proposed to do, and what the risks were. Wrapped in my towel at the door of the bathroom, I felt desperate and hopeful.

'Forty percent of children with this diagnosis also have other abnormalities. We will only do the surgery if the other parts of the body are working properly, and it makes sense to do it. So far, it looks good for Sophia, but we are waiting for a few final elements. Do you understand?'

It felt so wrong, so awful, to hear him talk about our daughter like she was a used car in for assessment of whether she was worth saving or not. But that was exactly what they were doing. I hated it, but I also understood it. We were in their hands. We had to trust them.

I nodded, blinking back my tears.

'Yes,' said Sean into the microphone.

'You must understand that even if all the rest of her parts are working, the connection may not be possible. We will only know if we have enough oesophagus to make the connection when we operate.'

My heart took off as if I had just done a 200-metre sprint. I felt dread in my gut. It wasn't only 'was she worth saving?' It was also, 'was it possible to save her?'

I felt my body prickle.

I heard Sean ask, 'Is there no way to extend it if there isn't enough?'

Dr Kapur's matter of fact answer, followed, far away, as if in a dream, 'No, for the moment there is no material that can match the human oesophagus. Given where we are today there are no replacement options.'

I felt the weight of what Dr Kapur had said settle onto me like a lead coat. The criticality of the length of the oesophagus had not been spelt out by Dr Murphy. Tears flooded. I had just washed away the last lot. The voices in the stairwell continued as I gripped onto the door jamb, feeling faint.

It was not as easy as it had seemed when Dr Murphy laid out the plan. First, they would not do the surgery if there were other serious malfunctions. Second, the length of Sophia's malformed oesophagus would decide life or death for her today, notwithstanding the other risks. I breathed deeply to keep the sobs at bay. I had to keep myself together.

'From the X-rays we are hopeful that we will have enough, but we have to make you aware of the risks. Do you understand?' asked Dr Kapur.

We had just spent the afternoon reading up on the situation and the risks. With his call I felt that we were fully informed. My eyes connected with Sean's, me at the top of the stairs and him at the bottom.

'Yes,' I said quietly.

'Yes,' said Sean into the mic.

'Sophia could go into surgery within the hour. You should come to the hospital now, so you can give your consent in person. But be available on the phone, in case she goes in sooner,' said Dr Kapur.

'We'll come straight away,' said Sean. 'We'll be there in half an hour.'

He hung up. I dressed hurriedly, then hugged Mam goodbye.

'God bless, Toots,' she said. 'I'll be praying for Sophia.'

Mam handed me a tissue and I wiped away the latest flush of tears.

As I opened the car door, Dr Kapur called on the mobile.

'Sophia's going into theatre. We need your consent,' he said. 'I'll read through the risks, and then you need to say you understand, and that you agree to the surgery.'

The cul-de-sac around which our house, and our neighbours' houses, were built, was quiet, save for a few birds twittering in the hedges nearby. Now the birdsong was joined by a voice from the mobile that Sean held up on speaker mode. I stood in the crook of the car door listening intently as Dr Kapur read the risks. I was the person who hid behind the sofa and blocked my ears for violent scenes in films. I felt like doing that. As what academics called a 'Highly Sensitive Person', someone who experiences acute physical, mental, or emotional responses to stimuli, every risk he read ricocheted through me. Despite having heard them from him earlier, and read them on the internet, hearing them now, specifically for our daughter, hit like a hammer. I felt dizzy.

We had to agree, there was no other option for Sophia. I was struck by how the world carried on around us. For us, everything had changed, the focus of our lives, what was important, everything.

'We agree, Dr Kapur,' said Sean.

'Good. She'll go into theatre soon, but if you hurry, you might see her pre-theatre.'

We leapt into the car hoping that we would. As we flew along the Rock Road adrenalin pumping through our veins, the tranquillity of our drive the previous day felt like a lifetime ago. A few minutes before reaching Temple Street Children's University Hospital, the phone rang again, and my body flooded with more adrenalin.

'Hello, Mrs Feely, it's Kathryn, a nurse from Intensive Care in Temple Street. You needn't hurry. Sophia's gone into theatre. It'll be a good few hours before she's out.'

I felt disappointed that we hadn't seen her before she went in, but it was good news, the sooner she was operated on the better.

'We're a few minutes away, so we'll come anyway,' I said. 'We want to be near her, even if we can't see her.'

'I understand,' said Kathryn. 'Call for me when you arrive.'

Reflecting on it, I wish I had insisted on staying with Sophia to go from Holles Street to Temple Street. Although she was sedated to unconsciousness, she knew our presence, especially mine, the familiar voice she had heard for nine months. I should have stayed with her. I hope hospitals allow parents, or at least the mother, who is their most familiar voice, to stay, to have as many precious moments as possible with their newborn, to let them know how loved they are.

CHAPTER EIGHT

Life critical surgery

We announced ourselves at Temple Street National Children's University Hospital reception then stood waiting for someone from ICU to fetch us.

'Don't you want to sit down, Caro?' asked Sean.

'I think I feel better standing.'

Our daughter's life was on a knife edge, I wasn't in a state to sit. A few minutes later, a young woman with a lively, friendly face, approached us. Her smile made me feel welcome and supported. It was a smile filled with compassion, the kind of smile that gave comfort in your darkest hour.

'You must be Sophia's mum and dad,' she said. 'I'm Kathryn.'

Sophia's mum and dad. We were Sophia's mum and dad. In the crisis of the last few hours, that news had been lost. I felt my eyes fill with emotion.

'As I said on the phone, Sophia's in theatre, so it'll be a few hours before you can see her. She's in good hands.' She paused and smiled reassuringly. 'Follow me. I'll show you to the ICU parents' waiting room.'

Kathryn led us out of reception, along a wide corridor, up a flight of stairs and into a passage that was like part of an old house, complete with creaking wooden floorboards. Like at Holles Street, it felt like we were transferring to a parallel universe. In a way we were, we were experiencing something we had never encountered before, that needed courage, and brought a depth of feeling hitherto unknown to us.

Kathryn opened one of the passage doors onto a small lounge that would have been welcoming if it had had warm light. A single cold fluorescent tube shone down on a sofa, two chairs and a coffee table. Kathryn pointed out the nearest toilets, then invited us to sit, and sat down herself.

She explained the surgery, drawing on a piece of paper, as she spoke. I was getting the impression that medical people liked to draw. It made it easier to understand and more intuitive than words alone. With each explanation and new artwork, we became more familiar with what was happening to our daughter.

'Phone me if you need anything,' she said, and wrote the extension on the piece of paper with the drawing. She laid it beside the black handset on the side-table. 'I'll call when we have an update.'

Then she was gone. We settled into the sofa, and I snuggled up under Sean's arm. A few minutes later, feeling the need for action, I reached for the pocket Bible I had brought, and read a few pages, then said a prayer for

Sophia. Praying felt like I was helping, there was comfort in it.

We attended the local Church of Ireland to be part of the community, to respect something that was tradition for both of us. We had immediate family, and extended family, that were strong Christians, and knowing they were praying for Sophia was reassuring. I believed in a great Spirit, something that united us, rather than religions that divided us. It wasn't only divisions between religions, it was divisions within religions. Since arriving in Ireland, I understood how deeply divided Christians could be, even among themselves. Northern Ireland was in the news constantly. I discovered horrors like knee capping listening to the radio in Dublin traffic.

Now, religious divisions forgotten, I prayed to all the mighty powers I had encountered, to the Great Spirit, to God, to Jesus. I beseeched them to spare Sophia.

Hours passed in silence. We were unable to talk, frozen by the sword hanging over our daughter, the length of her oesophagus. Sean bought sandwiches from the hospital shop. They tasted like cardboard. I had no appetite.

'We're guaranteed to lose weight if we stick around here for a while,' said Sean, trying to lighten the mood.

I couldn't eat. I couldn't read. I walked up the corridor to the toilet. I drank water. I went to the toilet again. I returned. I prayed. We sat, totally focused on our situation. It was like meditating but we didn't know to call it that.

The phone rang. We exchanged a glance of fear. Even if it was possible, the surgery was risky, Sophia could die undergoing it. We knew it. I leapt up and grabbed the phone. Reflecting on my reaction now, I see it was wrong.

If it had been bad news, they would never have phoned it through, but at the time I felt it could have been either way.

'It's Kathryn. I wanted to let you know the surgery is going well. I just got the news from a theatre nurse. The oesophagus was long enough to make the connection. They're about halfway.'

'Oh Kathryn, thank you so much,' I said, giving Sean a thumbs up, tears of joy distorting my vision. A similar feeling to when I had run a few kilometres, flowed through my body, a dose of endorphins.

'My shift is over so another nurse will be down to let you know when Sophia is out.'

'Thank you.'

I dropped onto the sofa, relief flooding through me. We embraced. We had been in a state of extreme stress knowing that it all depended on whether there was enough oesophagus. Now at least we knew it was possible. We basked in the good news. I called Mam and she promised to share it. There were still risks, but our daughter could be healed.

It was late morning across the Atlantic, on the west coast of Canada. My dad was on the road back from golf with a close friend, a doctor, a shoulder for him to lean on as we passed through this extreme moment. As he drove home, he prayed for Sophia. The clouds lifted off Mount Arrowsmith and the sun came out and lit up the snowy peaks. He felt like he was receiving a message from God that they had been able to make the connection. When he got home Mum's message confirmed it.

In the parents' waiting room, Sean and I slipped back into our meditative state. I walked up the corridor, the boards creaking in sympathy. I didn't feel pain when urine hit my wound. I didn't have tea tree oil or a jug to mix it into water. It was like the episiotomy wound no longer existed. Something far greater had become my focus, the need to protect our baby. We were feeling that powerful thing that Bev spoke of in Oxford a year before, deepest love, parental love.

We didn't know this baby in a relationship sense, since we had not had a chance to be with her since her birth, but that didn't matter. We loved her with a force that made me feel strong. It was a force so great, that I felt like we could have trekked across Ireland for her that night. We were powerful beyond measure in our parental love. But all we could do was wait. I drank more water. We sat in silence.

Hours later there was a knock on the door and another ICU nurse, Yvonne, introduced herself. Her face said good news and without hearing a word, I knew everything was okay.

'Sophia is in post theatre recovery,' she said. 'The surgeon, Prof. Puri, will be up in about half an hour to talk to you about the operation.'

She left us, clearly not as talkative as Kathryn.

The anxiety of the hours of waiting fell away like letting go of weights. I felt light as a feather. Sophia had made it through mammoth life-saving surgery. She had made it to this first critical milestone. We hugged, clinging together, feeling the fear dissolve, and relief and deep joy take its place. I called Mam. Talking about it made the success even more real and miraculous. Sophia was alive. She had been fixed. Mam took the news hungrily, eager to share it with family, friends, and even strangers, that were praying for Sophia. In our focus we had almost forgotten that there was a whole tribe beyond that lounge, who were on tenterhooks, some in distant time zones, who had stayed up through the night praying for her.

While we waited for the surgeon, I paced up and down the corridor. Eventually, tired by my pacing I sat back on the sofa to join Sean in renewed silence. At last, another knock. Yvonne was accompanied by a man with a round open face, a face that you knew was home to a kind person. Prof. Puri smiled warmly as we introduced ourselves and shook hands, then invited us to sit down.

'Overall, the operation went well,' he said. 'I'll explain what we did.'

He sat in the armchair opposite us and began to draw the surgery on a piece of paper on the low table between us.

'The top part of the oesophagus was a dead end, as we had seen on the X-rays. In theatre, we found the lower end of the oesophagus coming up from the stomach had attached itself to the trachea instead of to the top part of the oesophagus where it should have been. We detached the lower end of the oesophagus from the trachea, opened the upper dead end, and connected the two. The connection was tight, but possible. We have sewn the two together and the tissues should heal so that the two ends remain connected.'

He drew two ends connected by a web of stitches. As he spoke, his hands moved to draw or make a point. They were a young man's hands that didn't match his greying hair. His forearms were muscular, his hands veined and powerful. He had been working on our daughter for hours, his hands and forearms working with ultimate finesse on her neonatal being.

'Do you understand so far?'

'What's the trachea?' I asked.

'It's the windpipe, the tube that takes air to the lungs,' he replied.

I nodded. My bank of anatomical and medical terminology was growing at speed.

'There are risks with such a tight connection,' said Prof Puri. 'We have stretched the two parts to get them to meet. If the two parts don't heal properly then the oesophagus will leak, and we'll have to operate again.'

Sean and I exchanged a glance. Another session like tonight was too much to contemplate. He saw our look.

'There's a chance it will heal properly, and we won't need to. I have to make you aware of the potential risks. The rest of the body looked completely normal and was functioning perfectly,' he added to salve our fears.

'Do you have any questions for me?'

'If everything goes perfectly and there are no complications, how soon could she go home?' I asked, thinking ahead.

'Two weeks was the fastest recovery we've had,' he said.

Two weeks. We could have our baby home in two weeks. Until that moment I hadn't thought beyond this first step.

Seeing the delight on my face he added, 'But we aren't through the high-risk phase yet. The first three days after surgery are the most critical. If we get through that with no problems, then the next milestone is the X-ray to see if there are any leaks. We usually do that at around ten days.'

'If we get through that...' I felt fear and adrenalin flood my system again as the words ricocheted through me.

'Overall, we are satisfied with how things went. We were lucky that your daughter stayed inside longer than usual.

The extra weight gained in the ten days overdue helped her and will help her recovery too.' He paused a moment and smiled at us. 'Do you have any more questions for me?'

'No, I think we understand everything. Thank you so much Prof. Puri,' I said.

'Thank you,' said Sean.

We got up to shake his hand again, eyes glistening. Words and gestures could not express what we felt. He was a miracle worker, a giver of life. We saw them out of the lounge. Yvonne said a few words to Prof. Puri in the passage, then came back in.

'So how was that?' she asked.

'I feel relieved on one hand, and scared on the other,' I said.

'He seems like an incredible surgeon,' said Sean.

'He's the best of the best. Sophia's lucky to have him. He's a world-renowned specialist in this kind of neonatal surgery. But while what he said is accurate, I have to stop you getting your hopes up about being home in two weeks. That was the best possible outcome with everything as ideal as it could have been under the circumstances. It could be much longer than that. With complications it could be six months. Two weeks only happened once. Don't set your hopes on that.'

We nodded. I felt the knot of fear expand again.

'When can we see her?' asked Sean.

'She should be installed in ICU in about 20 minutes. We'll call you when it's okay to come up,' she said, and disappeared up the passage.

I felt an instinctive need to see Sophia like my body was pining for her. I called Mam to share the details from Prof. Puri's visit and told her not to stay up since we didn't know when we would be home. The world went quiet, the hospital settled into sleep mode. We waited. An hour later there was still no word, so I called the phone number Kathryn had left for us.

'Oh yes, you can come up,' said the Matron. 'We'd forgotten that you were waiting to see her. I'll send Yvonne for you now.'

I felt a little shaft of upset that they had forgotten us but reminded myself that they were caring for a ward of children that were fighting for their lives. We had no idea what life critical emergencies they had faced in the hour we had been waiting. Yvonne came down and took us up to ICU. We followed her instructions in the disinfection zone, washed our hands in orange antiseptic and donned disposable gowns and slippers. Inside, the ward was dim and quiet. Beds, cots, and incubators were placed at intervals around the large room.

Our stop was the first glass-sided cot. Sophia lay in it, magnificently alive after her first 24 hours of extreme conditions on planet Earth. Despite hours of surgery, she looked perfect, totally peaceful, and cherubic. Air and liquid were being fed to her by machines on either side of the tiny pod. A screen showed her heartbeat and her breathing. We would discover that any unusual activity on either would sound an alarm.

'I'll leave you for a few minutes,' whispered Yvonne.

We took in the sight of our daughter, exquisite joy. She was so tiny and vulnerable, a delicate gift that had almost slipped through our fingers, and still could. Too quickly, a light touch on my shoulder signalled it was time to leave.

I struggled to tear myself away. It was a miracle to be looking at our daughter alive and 'fixed'. I didn't want to leave in case there was a call in the night. Tears welled up as we walked away, and I swallowed hard. Sobbing in this peaceful night ward wouldn't help anyone. I flicked away my tears and followed Yvonne and Sean.

Out in the corridor, Yvonne gave us the information sheet for parents. The only things I remember from the rules were that we could visit as much as we wanted, and that we had to promise to follow the disinfection procedure. Visiting was all important. We needed to be with our daughter as much as possible.

Sean and I walked down the stairs, along the corridor, and out past reception as if in a dream. As we got into the car, the bell on the church opposite the hospital tolled midnight. Sean put the key into the ignition, then turned to me with tears rolling down his cheeks. I reached across, squeezed his arm, and leaned into his face, my tears joining his. Raw emotion poured out of us, there was no need for words. We cried in cathartic waves washing the stress out, and letting the hope in.

Eventually Sean backed out of the parking space and onto the deserted street. From the Children's Hospital to the Rock Road, we soared up and down a roller coaster of feelings, from joy at the good news of that night, to fear of the risks that lay ahead. By the time we got home, we had control of ourselves but seeing Mam at the door made me dissolve again. She hugged me with all her force.

'She's so beautiful Mam. I feel so scared that she'll be taken away from us.'

We stood in the entrance hall in a deep embrace.

Remembering the midwife's advice, I went upstairs to pour antiseptic tea tree oil mixed with water onto my wound that was still numb with shock. In bed I prayed deep gratitude for Sophia's successful surgery, and a plea for a safe passage through the night.

I woke up crying, painful sobs that came from the depths of my soul. For a moment I didn't know why. Then I remembered. I was home without my daughter. Instead of coming home with her the day before, we had left her in an Intensive Care Unit. Then I felt relief that we hadn't been woken by a phone call in the night. I called ICU to ask how she was.

CHAPTER NINE

Hope in the time of ICU

The nurse said Sophia was in good shape, she had made it through the first night after surgery with no hitches. We got ready as fast as we could, eager to see her. The drive in was easy, it was Sunday so no traffic. At Temple Street Hospital we followed the route upstairs and into the ICU border zone for the washing and dressing protocol. The smell of chlorine was in every corner of the hospital but in the small anteroom at the entrance to ICU, the aroma of the orange liquid antiseptic soap took the upper hand. We geared up in blue throwaway robes, masks, and shoe covers and waited at the door.

Matron O'Malley waved through the glass, then let us in and introduced herself. She escorted us to Sophia who was in the same place and position as the night before. The monitors showed perfect heart beats and breathing. I felt a wave of instinctive love for the tiny body in the cot.

Seated on either side of her we took on the first hospital day, soaring up mountains of hope and then down the other side into fear. When the valley of fear was too much, we went outside to cry quietly, not wanting it to touch Sophia or the rest of our ICU community with it. We read poetry and psalms. I sang quietly, songs about love, songs about home, about Ireland and South Africa.

We didn't talk to the other parents, each of us kept our solemn sadness and fragile hope to ourselves. We all knew the lives in ICU were hanging by a thread. We could not take more than our own story at that moment. But I prayed for the other motionless bodies in the ward, the other tearful faces that came and went like ghosts in the shadows behind me.

Around midday, Matron O'Malley interrupted our vigil.

'Oh Lord, you poor thing. You just gave birth, and you're sitting on that hard, wooden stool. Don't you want a padded chair? You must be in agony.'

I looked up surprised. There was no pain. Only a total focus on the tiny body in front of me.

'No, don't worry. I'm fine,' I said.

'Ah now, nonsense,' said Matron. 'Kathryn, would you get the poor woman a comfortable chair?'

Re-seated in a padded chair I felt better for her care, as much as for the actual comfort. Matron O'Malley exuded a 'can-do' attitude that instilled confidence. I felt happy that Sophia was in a place with her at the helm. At the same time, I felt a little frightened of her, like one would feel about a strict, but good, headmistress.

The hospital canteen lunch was roast chicken, classic Sunday fare, what we often shared with our friends Aideen and Barry whose son had been part of my baby education. Sunday roast chicken in their home in Monkstown was part of our Dublin life. They were our adopted family, stepping in for our blood family who were disconnected from us by distance. Mam had told them about Sophia, but we hadn't spoken yet. I wasn't strong enough to talk to anyone. It was all too raw. The canteen food was tasty, but I wasn't hungry. I felt listless, like there was pent-up energy that wasn't being used.

We continued our vigil at Sophia's bedside. The odd monitor went off, but they were false alarms, and everything swiftly returned to calm. As the day progressed, despite reading, singing, and praying, I began to feel helpless and useless. We weren't doing any of the usual things for our newborn daughter. No feeding, washing, changing. We were sitting. We were waiting. The ICU team took care of everything, their eight-hour shifts came and went in a behind-the-scenes dance that we were barely aware of.

Mid-afternoon we promised the tiny unconscious being that we would be back in the morning and packed up to go home. In Killiney, Mam had cleaned the house and planted some of the seedlings. Our local priest, a gentle, kind man, had called to find out if our baby had arrived. On hearing the story, he had taken Mam with him for the Sunday service and prayed for Sophia. People across the globe were praying for her. I felt thankful that our daughter was surrounded by so much love and prayer.

Aideen arrived with two bears and a card for Sophia. She hugged me and I dissolved into tears. I poured the previous 48 hours out in a torrent. It was the first time I had talked about the labour, birth, and our vigil at the hospital during the surgery. Aideen hugged me, a deep embrace of compassion. Talking to my friend gave me a sense that everything was going to be okay. Seeing that I was getting a grip on myself, Aideen put her 'organised mum' hat on.

'I know it's hard to think of this now, but if you want to breastfeed Sophia, you should consider expressing breast milk so she can feed when she's recovered. If you don't express now, the milk may not be there when she's ready to feed. Ask the hospital for help. Tell them if you want to breastfeed.'

I hadn't thought of that. No-one had mentioned it, not even the Domino midwives. I had an expressing machine that I had bought with a view to continuing breastfeeding when I went back to work, and Sophia started in crèche. We had booked a crèche near my office as soon as we knew we had a baby on the way. In Dublin you put your children on all the lists the minute they were conceived: crèche, primary school, even high school.

When Aideen left, I went upstairs and took the expressing machine out of its packaging. The complexity of putting it together was too much. I placed it straight back into its plastic bag. I wasn't ready. At the same time, I knew Aideen was right. Tears started to roll again. I put the express machine into the backpack with the books and other gear for the hospital, then wiped away my tears and went downstairs and out into the garden. I put my face to the sun and closed my eyes. Its orange reflection glowed through my eyelids. Its life-giving energy warmed my skin. Mam came out with a blanket and laid it on the grass.

'Lie down and look up at the sky, Toots,' she said. 'It'll do you good.'

I lay down and took in the blue, blue sky and the comforting sounds of home, birds in the garden, the odd soft sound of a car passing slowly through our quiet neighbourhood, distant waves on Killiney beach. I felt these familiar things surround me like a security blanket. Our lives were upside down, but life continued. It seemed strange but also comforting that it was so. I closed my eyes then opened them. Mam was silhouetted against the sun with our house behind her.

'Thanks Mam,' I said. 'You were right. I feel better already.' Lying on the grass looking at the sky was a pick-me-up that had proven itself many times.

'You relax there. You need it,' said Mam.

I looked at the sky, then back at her.

'I feel like I can dare to hope,' I said.

'Oh, Toots darling,' said Mam, eyes shining. 'I'll bring you a cup of tea.'

She returned with tea and the phone. It was my brother. Like other family, friends, and prayer circles around the globe, he was praying for Sophia. He had deep faith and a healing touch. Mam had already given him the basic story.

'It's better if you ask God for exactly what you want,' said Garth. 'Tell me exactly what we need to pray for now that the surgery is done.'

I explained what Prof. Puri had drawn and what he said: that the connection was tight, and complications were possible.

'We need the oesophagus top and bottom, that are sutured together by a fine web of stitches, to knit together. The two ends are held together by the stitching. They need to heal together perfectly. If any part is still open when they do the X-ray in ten days, she'll need more surgery.'

Tears began to flow again. The shock of what our daughter had been through was hitting home.

'Mrs Phlugg,' said Garth using his nickname for me, 'I pray for courage for you and Sean, and a fast recovery for Sophia.'

I knew he had a direct line to God. Hearing his words made me feel better.

'We also need to pray that she gets through these high-risk first three days post-surgery.' I swallowed hard and finished what I wanted to say. 'These three days are the highest risk for anyone coming out of surgery.'

'I'll pray for Sophia. Now I know exactly what to pray for, it'll be better, more precise. God bless you and Sean, and baby Sophia.'

He hung up.

Mam came out with a box of tissues. I lay back down on the blanket and cried; unstoppable tears poured out of me.

Sean clattered away in the kitchen making dinner for us. His Chartered Financial Analyst exam finals were coming up, but he couldn't study. It was impossible to think of anything but Sophia.

My sister Foo called. We talked and I cried. I cried so much sitting on that blanket under the blue sky that I was sure there were no more tears inside. I cried for the fears but also for the hope that Sophia would make it. Please God. Please let Sophia live.

CHAPTER TEN

Express yourself

The following day, taking the route into Temple Street with Sean and Mam, bumper to bumper traffic and screaming sirens reminded us that the working week had started. Our lives had become a vigil with no work week, everything focused on Sophia's recovery. We were daring to hope.

ICU only allowed two visitors at a time. Sean said hello to sleeping Sophia then tore himself away to drive across the city to his office. He had to share the news of our daughter's birth and explain that he needed longer paternity leave than expected. Instead of a couple of days, two weeks was required, and perhaps a lot more. Between visits to the washroom to regain his composure, he told his boss and his colleagues.

Leaving Mam with Sophia, I stepped out to call Frank, a close work colleague, so he could share the news with my work. Hearing the words about the operation coming out of my mouth made it so real, so hard, but also so miraculous. The connection had been possible. Sophia had made it through the first 24 hours post-surgery. I felt like shouting the magnificent news from the top of the steeple opposite the car park where the bell had tolled. I promised to keep him posted and hung up to regain control of my breathing.

On my return, the ward was buzzing. The day before, Sunday, there were few doctors and more visitors. Now there were doctors coming and going constantly, and hardly any visitors. The mid-morning doctors were satisfied with Sophia's progress. After they left, I decided to seize the day and follow up on Aideen's suggestion about expressing. I found the Matron at the main ICU counter.

'Matron O'Malley, I want to talk to you about something,' I said, feeling nervous.

'Sure pet, what is it?'

'I want to breastfeed.'

She looked up from her paperwork, surprised, perhaps even speechless. I filled the empty space.

'What does a mother in my situation do?'

'Oh! Of course, dear, I think we've a person in the hospital that can help you. I'll call and see if she's on duty today. If she is, I'll ask her to pop in to see you.'

Her mannerisms reminded me of Robin Williams' Mrs Doubtfire.

'Thank you. My friend, who's a breastfeeding counsellor, says it's important to start as soon as possible.'

'I'll call to find out right away then,' she said, and picked up the phone.

I felt bad concerning busy ICU staff with something that seemed like a non-necessity, a nice-to-have. In a place where children's lives were touch and go, breastfeeding wasn't a priority. Without Aideen, I wouldn't have thought of, or had the courage, to broach the subject. Despite being a confident IT professional in my mid-thirties, in the hospital I felt like a child that knew nothing, that had to listen to the adults around me about what was right, and what was to be done. I felt like I should only speak when spoken to like a good little kid. What a wrong sensation. Follow your intuition and speak up even if you are a medical dunce.

Alexandra Fuller's memoir 'Leaving before the rains come' delivers this message. In the book her ex-husband has a nearly fatal fall off a horse. In the ensuing hospital scenes, if Fuller hadn't been there to fight for his life, he would likely have died. Our intuition and instinct can sometimes offer better diagnosis than medical knowledge. Don't stand back, make your voice heard.

The Matron was good to her word. Susan, the breastfeeding aide, arrived within an hour. She had short red hair and a lean body. She exuded an air of 'get on with it'. There was no messing about with chit chat.

'So, you want to breastfeed?' She said, then raced on before I answered. 'Good for you. We don't often get that request from ICU mums, but we'll do everything we can to support you. When your baby is off the machines and able to feed, you can stay in the hospital free of charge. We'll give you vouchers for meals too.'

'That's very generous,' I said, not daring to think so far ahead.

'I brought you some sterile jars to express into. Each express should go into a separate jar and be given to the nurses. When you need more, let them know.'

I jotted her words down in my diary.

'Do you have an expressing machine?' she asked.

'Yes,' I said. 'I have it with me, but I don't know how to use it.'

'I'll show you,' she said.

I pulled the apparatus out of the backpack. She took it and put it together for me, then quickly showed me what to do.

'Have a go. Any problems let me know. I'll drop in to see how you're doing tomorrow.'

Still not sure about what to do, I took the machine and went into a side room that Matron said I could use. It was a tight space. I felt like I was in a masturbation cubicle without the Playboy magazines. The sucker of the express machine pinched my nipple. It was painful and unpleasant. After milking both breasts I had a few dribbles of yellow liquid, enough to line the pipes but not enough to even bother putting into a sterilised jar. Now I would have to clean and sterilise the equipment for no result. I felt a failure. I called Aideen.

'Well, for a start, it probably isn't worth using the express machine at this early stage. Just express by hand straight into the jars. The quantity of yellow stuff, colostrum, is always minuscule. Don't be put off, it's a critical part of your milk production. It will boost Sophia's immunity. Don't throw it away even if you only get a few drops,' she encouraged.

'How do I express by hand?' I asked.

'Gently massage the nipple then squeeze it to get the milk to drip into the jar,' replied Aideen. 'When the colostrum is finished, and the milk is flowing, it will jet into the jar. Don't be discouraged. You'll figure it out. It takes time.'

I went back into the cubicle to try again. I remembered hand milking cows at a neighbour's farm when I was growing up. I just had to do the same. At least this time there was no risk of being kicked in the head. I gripped my right breast with my left hand and massaged it gently, bent over the jar, intent not to lose a drop of the precious gold. After milking the other side, a thin layer lined the bottom of the container. I handed it to the nurse proudly.

'We'll need a bit more than that,' she said, deflating me.

I called Aideen again. She worked full time as a management coach, but she found a way to take my calls immediately at that critical time. She was my lifeline.

'How much should I be producing?' I asked.

'Whatever you can,' she said. 'Don't worry about the nurse. She probably never breastfed or advised on it. You saw the Matron's reaction; a breastfeeding mum is a rare beast in ICU. No one would have more colostrum than that. Ignore her. The most important thing is to keep expressing. Just think how important each jar is to Sophia's recovery, no matter how small. To be scientific about it, you need to produce about two teaspoons per hour to feed a newborn. You should express every couple of hours or so, like a tiny baby would feed. They can drink around two tablespoons at a single feed at three days old, double that at a week and double that again at a month.'

I wrote Aideen's wisdom diligently into my notebook. She was my guru. Without her I would have given up. Without her I wouldn't have even started.

Back in ICU, Mam was reading the Bible quietly to Sophia. I sat down in my comfort chair and looked around. The large room had sash windows and felt like part of a manor house, not a hospital. I liked the ambiance. It was so much better than a clinical modern structure. My mind began to wander. I felt more normal, like everything was going to be okay. Outside a bright day demanded we get out, so we took turns to go for a walk in the sun.

We were back in our chairs when the young registrar, Vivan, visited on his rounds. I had met him the previous day and found him easy going and friendly. I introduced him to Mam.

'Very pleased to meet you, Mrs Feely,' he said.

'Thanks Vivan, my mum's Mrs Wardle,' I corrected.

'Call me Lyn,' said Mam.

'Mum was a midwife and a matron in her day,' I said proudly.

'Well Sophia's doing well. The only anomaly is a slight heart murmur. We have ordered an ECG and the specialist cardiologist will check it tomorrow,' said Vivan.

The blood drained from my head. Everything was not okay. Sophia had a heart murmur. We had read that this was relatively common with the sort of malformation she had. I felt dread like lead.

Seeing my face pale, he added, 'We're not too concerned about it. We have to check it given the concerns about other problems for babies with this condition but please don't worry.'

I felt like screaming, 'Don't worry? You just told me Sophia has a heart murmur!'

My heart raced, readying me for fight or flight, I closed my eyes then opened them and saw him disappear through the staff door. On the phone a few minutes later, Sean calmed me.

'We have to wait to see what the specialist says, perhaps it's nothing. If it's something, then we will deal with it when the time comes,' he said.

Talking to Sean was like talking to Yoda from Star Wars. He gave me perspective. Walking always helped when I was worried about something, so I went for another walk. The beach would have been better than the busy streets around Temple Street, but it was walking.

Feeling a little more serene, I returned to ICU. Sophia looked so peaceful. The heart rate machine showed perfect beats. It was hard to believe there was a problem. I gave Mam a squeeze and sat down. My emotions soared up and down again like they had the first day.

At the hospital canteen with trays in hand and plates loaded, we found a free table and sat down. I felt a little dizzy. The information about the heart murmur had sent me reeling. I took a bite, chewed, and swallowed, then looked up and our eyes connected. I felt a welling of emotion that I couldn't stop.

'Oh Mam, she's still so fragile. The heart murmur has made me feel like she's slipping through our fingers,' I said, and tears started to roll down my cheeks.

'I know, Toots,' said Mam taking my hand and squeezing it tight.

'I want her to stay so badly. When Vivan said "heart murmur" I felt like the air had been punched out of me.

Each day I get more attached to her. I can't bear the thought of losing her,' I said. I took an ever-ready tissue from my pocket and wiped my face. 'I keep reminding myself to be grateful that we have her, even if it's only for a short time.'

A sob rose up. There was a release in saying it. There was no point in being anxious about it. What would be, would be. I had to take the joy we had been given and be deeply grateful no matter what. It was easier to say than to do.

'Oh, Toots darling,' said Mam. 'We have to keep praying that she recovers quickly and that the heart murmur is a false alarm.'

I nodded and reached for another tissue.

'We need to be strong and positive,' I said.

'Yes darling, we need to be positive but it's also good to talk about your feelings,' said Mam squeezing my hand again.

The canteen was somewhere in the great middle of the building. There was no sun streaming in, just cold fluorescent light. The smell of over-boiled vegetables and instant gravy pervaded the space. Despite my lack of appetite and misgivings about the aromas, the fare was hearty. The cottage pie was tasty, as were the limp mixed vegetables alongside it. We ate quickly, not wanting to leave Sophia for long. Being away from ICU, and with Mam, allowed me to talk freely about my fear. I felt better for it.

Sophia was kept immobile by sedation so that the surgery wouldn't be disturbed. She was strapped down and loaded with wires and tubes, no clothes on save for a tiny nappy. Her tiny arms had splints on them to stop the tubes attached to her veins from moving. Compared to when we left for lunch, her head was angled in a different direction and her tiny legs were splayed out a little further.

As we settled in, Kathryn came over.

'I changed her nappy and moved her a little. It's important to do that from time to time, or her head will be flat on the part she was lying on. It's not normal for a baby to lie still twenty-four hours a day like this. But we can't move her too much because of the operation, just ever so slightly.'

I nodded. She couldn't move because part of her really *was* hanging together by a thread, a very carefully woven and magical thread.

Mam caught the train home and Sean joined me for the afternoon. He had handed his work over to colleagues. His boss had said to take as long as he needed. Their thoughts and prayers were with us. Jim, our local priest, visited to pray with us, and bless Sophia. I felt reassurance from his visit. A large bunch of flowers arrived from my work colleagues. My eyes filled with emotion at the love and support we were experiencing.

I expressed more colostrum. Now, no matter how small, each jar felt like I was doing something. I was contributing to Sophia's recovery. Instead of feeling useless, I felt useful. It gave my presence sense and a feeling of being needed. Expressing breast milk helped me cope with the desolation of not being able to touch my baby and the fear I experienced each time I thought about how fragile the life in the glass-sided cot was.

At home that evening, we toasted our three-day old daughter with Mam. With each passing day I felt a little more secure about her future. A key milestone was looming. The following evening Sophia would pass the 72-hours after surgery mark.

That night, before going to bed, I tried to express but couldn't. My breasts would not liberate any golden bounty. I gave up and went into a fitful sleep.

There was no call in the night. As I made my morning tea, I felt excited at the prospect of going into hospital to see Sophia. Then I remembered the heart murmur and felt leaden. I stopped what I was doing and prayed 'Please God. Please let the heart murmur be a false alarm.' I had to get a handle on my emotions. Feeling anxiety and fear over something that I had no control over, and that was not even confirmed, was wasting my energy. I took a few deep breaths. Mam looked around the door, still in her nightie.

'Hello Toots, how are you?' she asked.

'Good. I slept okay,' I said modifying the truth to stay upbeat. I gave her a kiss and a hug. 'How about you?'

'Not so good. My arthritis is playing up. I didn't sleep very well.'

'I'm so sorry Mam. Why don't you get dressed while I make your tea? It's too cold to wander around in a nightie, you know how low we keep the thermostat.'

Mam hadn't said it, but it was clear I wasn't the only one worrying about the heart murmur.

With Mam better dressed for the temperature in the house we sat down at the dining table. Andrew's fig cutting was pushing out its first green shoots. Six months before, it had been a seemingly lifeless branch. It was a sign of the power of the will to grow and live.

We sipped our tea and talked about Sophia, how we loved her, how delicate she was, about the seedlings in our tiny green house, which ones could be planted out, and what else Mam could do that day, so she didn't go mad all alone with the worry.

I expressed the tiniest dribble, then Sean and I left for the hospital. I wondered if my breastfeeding mission was doomed to failure. The milk wasn't increasing like Aideen had said it should.

At the hospital, Kathryn was sitting next to Sophia stroking her fine hair as gently as a summer breeze. She was an extraordinary nurse; professional but filled with love. We felt it and with it a sense of gratitude and security that Sophia was in loving hands.

'You can stroke her forehead,' she said. 'It's important for her to have touch even though she's unconscious.'

She showed me.

'Try it yourself. Yes, like that. Don't be frightened. You have sterilised your hands so there is little risk but great benefit from your touch.'

I touched Sophia's tiny forehead. It was warm and her skin was perfectly smooth and velvety. It was three days since I had touched her. She was like a gift wrapped in a glass-sided cot and with that electric touch I felt like I was opening the gift. Love surged through me. My breasts throbbed.

A few minutes later I stepped out to the cubicle to express, and the yellow liquid flowed freely. I barely needed to milk the nipples. Breastfeeding was emotional. Just touching Sophia for a moment created a lake of colostrum compared to my initial attempts. I presented my golden offering to a different nurse. This one took it gently as if it was more precious than diamonds.

'You are doing such a good thing for your baby,' she said.

Her gesture and words boosted my breastfeeding confidence and helped motivate me. I was fragile like Sophia, nothing like the solid mother figure of popular imagination.

Back in ICU, Kathryn was with Sean at Sophia's side.

'Hi Caro, I was just updating Sean. We've changed Sophia's drip from a post-op IV to a TPN IV, that's total parental nutrition intravenous.'

She got up to allow me to take her place and moved to the back of the cot.

'She's doing well. She's so beautiful.'

'Thank you, Kathryn,' I said, eyes shining with gratitude for her love and her words.

'It's so good that you are expressing. Sophia has a tube posted through her nose down the oesophagus and into her stomach so that milk can be passed directly to her stomach once the doctors are sure it's safe to do that. We'll start as soon as they give the green light.'

I felt a pop of excitement. We were on the road to recovery. The milk would serve a purpose. It would help Sophia get well. Through the day, the expressed milk changed from yellow to cream and increased in volume. Every four hours, a team of specialists including the registrar, anaesthetist, surgeon, and paediatrician, visited to check the patient's progress.

'We're planning to do a blood transfusion today to raise your baby's haemoglobin levels,' said Vivan.

'What about the heart murmur?' I asked.

'The cardiologist will be around this afternoon, but don't worry, she's doing very well.'

With the threat of a heart disorder hanging over Sophia, how could we *not* worry?

More flowers arrived from clients, friends, and family. They couldn't come into ICU, so they piled up in the parents' room. Sean's parents sent a small pink bear and a rag doll. A super fine hand-knitted blanket arrived from my grandmother Gigi, light as a feather and soft as a dove. Kathryn said we could put the bear and the blanket into the cot with Sophia.

By that third day, we knew the route and the hospital. Getting around was becoming instinctive. With everyday things familiar, and the crisis bubble thinning, I was able to see more of what was happening around us. In ICU, each patient had a dedicated nurse at any given moment. Sophia had four nurses taking care of her in shifts. I was becoming aware of how much work they were doing for Sophia.

A key indicator of a functioning body was urinating normally, so the medical staff tracked it to the millilitre. To quantify it they had installed a catheter. That day Sophia bypassed the catheter. I watched as Kathryn changed the tiny nappy.

'I'll have to refit the catheter,' said Kathryn. 'Tomorrow, if everything is going well, we'll take the catheter out and she'll need to be changed more regularly.'

Sophia was four days old, and I hadn't changed her nappy.

The paediatrician from Holles Street visited as part of his regular rounds to Temple Street on weekday afternoons. He checked the charts next to Sophia then looked up at us.

'Her progress is good,' he said.

I couldn't bear it anymore. I asked the crucial question.

'What about the heart murmur?'

'Oh that, oh, nothing to worry about. Many newborns have tiny anomalies like the one we saw.'

Sean gripped my hand in happiness. I felt like I was on top of Kilimanjaro, joyful and free.

'Thank you, Dr Murphy.'

'Yes, well, the team probably shouldn't have even worried you by mentioning it.'

Perhaps Vivan had felt he could talk to us like medical professionals after hearing Mam had been a matron in a hospital. In a way it was better to be fully informed but, in another way, perhaps we would have been better off in the dark, given it could have been nothing, as it turned out to be.

I went outside and called Mam. We revelled in the news that Sophia's heart was perfect. When we got home, we discovered the good news had propelled Mam through a productive afternoon. She had planted out the seedlings, washed everything possible, and made our dinner.

That evening, Sophia passed the 72-hour mark. I woke up feeling as sunny as the day was. At Temple Street ICU a 'Certificate of Bravery: awarded to Sophia Feely' hung above her cot. I reached for Sean's hand and our glistening eyes met. Sophia had made it to the second key milestone.

CHAPTER ELEVEN

Instinct and recovery

'Congratulations Sophia!' said Vivan when he came around.

Behind him, the sun streamed through the sash windows as if reinforcing the good news with its happy rays. Sophia looked so tranquil in her glass-sided cocoon.

'We've started weaning down the anaesthetics. The morphine was switched off last night and the Medazlin is being reduced every six hours. Later today we'll take out the epidural that is the local anaesthetic. This evening we'll turn off the ventilator. With the reduction of the anaesthetics, she'll be able to breathe on her own,' he said.

Sean and I listened carefully, and I took notes. Until then we had no idea of the technicalities of what they were doing to manage Sophia's recovery. We arrived, we prayed, we meditated, we took information given. Now we nodded, medical dunces on a crash course.

'We started Sophia on your breast milk today. We're giving her 5 millilitres per hour to begin with. That'll increase slowly and we'll reduce the TPN to match. You're doing a wonderful thing for your daughter. Research shows recovery is faster with breast milk.'

His words re-energised me to express. Knowing Sophia was getting the milk I was producing provided motivation, it was a good feeling.

'You'll have to up your production to keep pace or we'll have to complement the breast milk with formula,' he added.

I resolved to make more milk. As soon as Vivan had finished, I stepped out to call Aideen.

'What can I do to up my production?' I asked.

'You could try expressing more often, and maybe keep going for a bit longer even when the milk has stopped flowing,' said Aideen.

After careful disinfection of my hands, I took a sterilised jar and went into the cubicle to express. The act was becoming more familiar. I preferred expressing by hand to the pump. In fact, I hated the pump. It was messy, it needed sterilisation and it squeezed unnaturally. There was no emotion. Breastfeeding needed emotion, a feeling of connection. It was hard to do with a machine. I wondered how machine milked cows were conned into milking so freely. Perhaps the industrial suction pads had mimicked the feeling of a calf sucking or the cows had got used to it. They had not succeeded with my breast pump. But what did I know? I had yet to breastfeed a baby. It sounds so strange to milk yourself by hand. It was strange, quite freaky, but I had to do it. I felt like it helped me to stay strong, I was expressing for Sophia, but also for me. It gave me a sense of purpose.

Having milked myself dry, I took my offering to the nurse on duty, and she prepared to put it onto the drip feed that was going into Sophia.

'Shouldn't you be giving her the frozen colostrum first?' I asked.

'No, freshest is best,' she said.

'I don't think so. I think you need to defrost the yellow milk that I first expressed and give that to her first. It's the one most packed with immunity magic.'

She looked at me like I had just flown in on a broomstick.

'No, I don't think so. Freshest is best, but I'll call the breastfeeding nurse to check,' she said.

'Good idea.'

As a medical dunce I didn't feel qualified to tell a nurse how to do her job but, in this instance, I knew I was right. I felt desperate that the level of knowledge of this fundamental human act was so low. An hour later the milk supply pocket was filled with gold.

This day, like the other days, passed in a haze of doctors' visits, prayers, and meditation over the tiny form in the glass-sided cot, but there was something different, a sense of hope and excitement that was palpable, even from the nursing staff.

The following day, when Vivan came on the first of his rounds, he explained the next steps.

'Sophia's doing so well that we plan to move her out of ICU and into the high dependency ward, perhaps tomorrow. After that, the next big milestone is the X-ray to check if there are any leaks. We usually do that around ten days after surgery.'

'Is she ready for moving?' asked Sean. We had come to trust the ICU nurses. We felt secure. We didn't want her to move to somewhere new with less support.

'Absolutely she's ready. She's recovering incredibly quickly. That's partly thanks to your wife's breast milk. We know it makes a difference,' said Vivan.

'Then why isn't it encouraged more?' I asked without specifically referring to the incidents I had experienced. If my best friend wasn't a breastfeeding counsellor, I wouldn't be doing it, no matter how much I wanted to. It was difficult to do and difficult to motivate myself without a baby clamouring for feeding and someone reminding me it was so much better than formula. It was tough, but it was a lifeline for both of us. It helped my daughter and gave me purpose.

'It's a question of priorities, I guess. For the moment, hospitals like us haven't put effort into breastfeeding awareness. Babies are only a small part of the children we treat.'

At home that evening, Mam and I went for a walk on the beach while Sean made dinner. We felt free. Sophia had made it past the three-day mark with no complications, her heart had been certified perfect by the cardiologist, and she was ready to move out of ICU. As we walked Killiney's shore of sand and pebbles I felt so light I could have flown into the air and soared across the sky. The smell of fresh seaweed floated on a cool breeze. Wavelets broke on the pebbles, making sounds like soothing meditation music. A man hit a tennis ball for his golden retriever. The dog raced for it, bouncing with joy. I smiled, sharing it.

We turned for home. Out on the bay, a couple of kayakers paddled bravely towards Bray Head, its great bulbous promontory reaching into the sea in the distance. Two people deep in discussion passed us walking in the opposite direction. I wondered what their story was. Had they, like us, been through a week like no other?

Despite all the good news, that night I struggled to express. It was as if my body was doing the opposite of what my head was demanding. Sitting on the bed I milked a thimble full and the following morning as well. There was some frozen supply, but I had to get on top of this, if I wanted to avoid Sophia going onto formula. I resolved to express more frequently, to get up in the night and early in the morning. It would help me to get into the routine that would be necessary when she was breastfeeding.

But getting up without a baby to feed wasn't easy. The next morning, I found that I had turned the alarm off in the night and gone back to sleep. I expressed as soon as I woke up, admonishing myself. After brushing my teeth and washing my face I went downstairs and made tea, then took a cup up to Mam to wake her. She was coming in with us that day as Sean had to go into work for a few hours.

'Good morning, Mam,' I said and put the hot cup on the bedside table. 'How are you feeling?'

'Hello, Toots,' said Mam raising herself up and putting a cushion behind her back. 'Thanks, darling. I'm feeling much better than yesterday. I took a strong anti-inflammatory, so I slept well. Knowing Sophia's little heart has the 'all clear' helped.'

'Me too,' I said, putting my cup on the windowsill, then hopping onto the end of the bed. 'I set the alarm to express in the night, but I was in such a deep sleep I turned it off and slept right through.'

'You needed it,' said Mam and reached out to stroke my hand. 'The main thing is to keep expressing. Once Sophia is breastfeeding your production will increase naturally. You need to go easy on yourself.'

'But she'll soon be waking me for real, so I need to get into the rhythm.'

'Don't worry, Toots, it will happen naturally when she's here.'

I nodded and took a sip of tea.

'I feel a little anxious about her changing wards,' I said.

'They wouldn't move her if she wasn't ready, Toots.'

'I know, but it's hard to leave Kathryn and the amazing people in ICU.'

'You're right. They have been amazing,' said Mam. 'But the new team will be good too.'

'Thanks Mam. I know.' I took another sip. 'It helps to verbalise my thoughts – even the ones I know are not logical.'

We sat sipping tea in silence, then I got up and gave Mam a hug.

'We'd better get ready so you can have a couple of hours with Sophia before your lunch date.'

Brigid, my no-nonsense, 'pick the chips off the sidewalk and eat them' friend, had invited Mam for a girls' lunch that day.

Sean dropped us into hospital. Mam and I settled into our seats either side of Sophia's cot and took turns to stroke her tiny forehead. I went out to express soon after we arrived, keen to make up for time lost in the night. Being with Sophia made it so much easier than when I was at home without her.

Knowing it was her last day in ICU, the place had a special poignancy that morning. Parents, with shocked teary faces, in the state that we had been in the first day, came in, and took up their vigil next to a bed on the far side of the ward. I closed my eyes and said a prayer for them and their child. I took over stroking Sophia's forehead and focused on positive thoughts. When I checked my watch and my notebook, it was time to express.

Sean was coming up the stairs as I exited the cubicle. The timing was perfect, it was almost midday, Mam's lunch rendezvous. Sean took up a pew next to the cot, and Mam and I went down to reception. Brigid came through the main entrance, her auburn hair streaming out behind. She looked mighty, and full of potential. She was overdue by a few days, playing the waiting game like I had. She hugged me.

'Congratulations, Caro. Sophia is so beautiful. She looks like a porcelain doll.'

Sean had sent a photo and news of Sophia to close friends and family on Monday.

Brig looked at me fiercely and her eyes filled with tears. 'Oh Caro, I'm so sorry. If there's anything Sen and I can do, you know you can call. Anything.'

'Thanks, Brig,' I said and wiped my eyes with an ever-ready tissue.

'Are you sure you don't want to come with us, Toots? Sean is with Sophia. Maybe you should take a break,' said Mam.

'I need to be here,' I said. 'They're moving her to the new ward, I don't want to miss that. I wish I could be in two places at once. Have a great lunch you two. Good luck for the big day Brig!'

Seeing them off, I felt a pang of missing normal life, life that included friends and outings, rather than a daily hospital vigil. But I knew I wouldn't enjoy being elsewhere, this was where I needed to be, for me, and for Sophia.

Back in the ward I saw Sophia cry for the first time. The anaesthetics were wearing off. She was still well sedated so she wouldn't damage herself, or the tubes and IVs going in and out of her, but she was obviously feeling something.

'Nothing to worry about,' said Kathryn. 'She's starting to feel a little. It's normal for a baby to cry.' She gave her another dose of paracetamol.

'Why don't you two go off for lunch? Take your time. We'll transfer her to the new ward while you're gone. You'll find her in the St. Michael's High Dependency Unit after lunch.'

'That means we won't come back here,' I said. 'We'll miss you, Kathryn.'

'I'll miss you, and the little dote,' she said. 'She's recovering so well. You're doing well too. You being here and the breast milk are so important to her recovery. It's great that she's moving on so fast.'

We hugged goodbye, hearts brimming with gratitude and love. Kathryn was an exceptional nurse. We felt blessed to have had her at Sophia's side. In the disinfection chamber I took a last look back at Sophia's little cot and ICU, then Sean and I went down for lunch.

After chicken and vegetable curry, we found Sophia's new home. St. Michael's B High Dependency Unit was larger than ICU. It included babies, like Sophia, that were recovering from surgery or mishap at birth, and long-term high-dependency toddlers, children with disability that meant they were high-dependency for life. Instead of a nurse per patient, as there had been in ICU, there were two nurses for eight patients.

One of the nurses showed me a cubicle where I could express. The afternoon passed slowly. I found it hard to adjust to the new environment. It was a more modern room and felt darker than ICU. I didn't feel confident with the nurses yet. I felt like I needed to check everything they were doing. They had so many patients to care for, it was hard to see how they could do their jobs effectively.

There were fewer visitors. For the long-term patients, the families' lives had to continue, they had to earn a living. I felt desperately sad for those tots and their families. I tried to express, going through the motions every couple of hours, but expressing milk was not possible for a sad person. I was back on an emotional roller coaster. At home expressing was even more difficult. That night after a dismally small yield I called Aideen.

'I am a depressed cow,' I said. 'A depressed cow cannot be milked.'

Aideen and I laughed at the image, a potential scene for a Gary Larson Far Side cartoon.

'I know it's hard Caro. Keep thinking of Sophia. Breastfeeding is emotional. It's the love bond that releases the milk not just the milking action. It's important to her recovery.'

'I know Aideen, but I can't help it. I don't know why I'm depressed. I should be so happy that Sophia is making such good progress.'

'You are happy she is progressing, but you are exhausted. What you have now is possibly mild postnatal depression. Many people have it, even in perfect conditions. Until now you have been focused on the crisis. You have been ignoring your needs. But you need to look after yourself. Make sure you do things for your own happiness. Take a walk on the beach before you go to the hospital. Get some sun to perk you up and get some vitamin D into your system. Have a chat with your GP as well and tell her how low you feel.'

Aideen was onto something. Vitamin D was necessary for me and for my baby through the milk I provided to her. Getting outside always made me happier despite often feeling resistant to it especially if the weather wasn't perfect.

'You're right, it's been a week, and I've only had one walk on the beach.'

'There you go. You must look after yourself to be able to be a good mother. That will be true when Sophia is home too, not just for now.'

'Thanks Aideen.'

Her voice took on her organised Aideen persona.

'Now, to get back to the expressing problem. We must make it more real for you even when you're away from her. Perhaps you need a photo of Sophia, and something that smells of her, maybe a blanket she has had in her cot. Symbols like that will remind you of her, when you're at home and should help make the milk flow.'

'That sounds so weird,' I said.

'Not weird, instinct and love, with a side of biology and hormones,' said Aideen.

I was willing to try anything. With Sophia on the mend, I had to get myself, and my milk production, in order. My world revolved around expressing. Even walking on the beach now had a purpose beyond my wellbeing: vitamin D for my baby. Providing milk and contributing to Sophia's recovery had helped me cope with the crisis so far, to feel wanted instead of dissolving into depression. It was for both of us.

As I got used to the new ward, I realised how incredible these nurses were too. Despite the work load they were upbeat and joyful, willing and positive, like the sun coming out. I felt awe at their greatness of spirit, their giving and kindness.

CHAPTER TWELVE

X-rays and ecstasy

Sophia was six days old when I held her briefly for the first time since Dr Murphy had taken her away from me, that chilly Saturday morning. We pushed a chair up against the cot so we wouldn't disturb the tubes attached to her, then Mags, the nurse on duty, gently placed her in my arms. She was so small. Inside the cot, she looked bigger. Sleeping in my arms, I realised how tiny she was, her head a little larger than a tennis ball and covered with a smattering of down-soft hair. I was struck by her fragility, and by her might, the strength she had to pass through all she had already undergone in her short life.

I savoured the moment, closed my eyes, and breathed in her baby smell, aromas of homeliness like apples and fresh baked bread, with a touch of hospital. Sean stood by my side his hand gently on my shoulder. The world stopped. We became a circle of love. I felt a deep connection; she was part of me but her own person. The deepest love that Bev had talked about, flowed through me. It was something that could not be explained or reasoned. It was. A moment of pure bliss.

The moment was interrupted by Mags telling me to transfer Sophia to Sean. Her excursions from her cot were strictly timed. We transferred her carefully, keeping the tubes in their positions. Sean took her gently. His face began to glow, radiating the love and happiness that comes from holding your newborn close.

Those few minutes felt like a stolen kiss, a sweet moment snatched. We couldn't risk damaging her delicate surgery. The miracle of healing needed tranquillity. She woke every now and then but was still heavily sedated so that she wouldn't pull the tubes out, something any normally active baby would have done. She had to stay somewhat calm until X-ray day.

X-ray day. It was out there, like a beacon, and a threat. If that went well, I would start breastfeeding like a normal mother. If not. I didn't want to think about that.

'We'll be stopping the IV soon so Sophia can be exclusively on milk,' said Mags.

'That's great news,' I said.

'We're preparing for her to feed normally if the X-ray goes well. But at the rate you're producing we'll have to supplement with formula. You're only providing about half of what we need. You need to up your production.'

Easy to say, but not so easy to do. Following Aideen's advice, I took the tiny blanket Gigi had knitted that had been in the cot for several days. It would be my source of Sophia's smell. The patchwork of pastel colours, 10-centimetre squares knitted from super fine yarn, was like a veil when held up to the light. It smelt of Sophia, that wonderful baby smell that fills your heart with sensations of home. It was like a messenger. I felt Sophia and Gigi through it. En route home, we stopped at Aideen's place for a print of a photo she had taken of Sophia.

'The photo and blanket will make a difference,' said Aideen. 'You'll be grand. You'll see. But don't put yourself under pressure. Remember whatever mother's milk you give Sophia is a bonus, no matter how small. Once she's feeding, it will build up naturally. The key is to keep it flowing until she's able to feed, even a small amount.'

Aideen was so wise. Everything she said was so perfect, and so perfectly timed. That night I installed myself in our bed, a pillow pushed behind me. A train line and open land separated our house from a sewage treatment plant and the beach. The window was ajar. I could hear the sea and the odd train passing. I had worried about the noise of the trains when we bought the house, but we got used to it. We hardly noticed the sound except in the garden, where it was too loud to miss. That evening, with night falling, I could see into the train carriages packed with commuters returning home to normal lives. Our lives would return to normal one day. For now, each day was a celebration of Sophia's life, of her making it to the next, of praying that she would.

I placed the photo next to me and breathed deeply into the blanket. It smelt so much of baby Sophia. I felt my uterus contract and my breasts tingle. Two fat tears rolled down my cheeks. I felt so sad that she wasn't with me, that she was going through this much pain and trauma so early in her life; that she could be taken away in the blink of an eye. I told myself being a wimp would help nobody. I thought of how wonderful it would be when she was home. I sniffed deep into the blanket again and looked at the photo. With a sterile jar in hand, I milked each breast. It was the best yield ever. Aideen was a genius. At this rate, we would stop the formula in no time.

The next day Sophia was doing so well that Mags disconnected the monitors and placed her onto my chest for an hour. I had a longing, a need to have her close, to snuggle her, but I had to be careful not to knock any tubes out of place. There could be no active cuddling, no movement, just breathing in and out, and feeling her breath, a meditative cuddle. I sank into extreme bliss, the kind you feel in the depths of an ecstatic meditation. Her baby smell, like hops and apple pie, her soft, velvety skin, the slight pressure of her against my heart, downy soft hair caressing my chin as I bent my head to kiss her, the sensation of love was almost too much to bear. Deepest love. Just thinking about that sensation now, decades later, fills me with a sense of bliss in my belly. This is deep, instinctive, emotion; something beyond our logical comprehension.

That day was Good Friday, so the hospital was quiet. Jim, our local priest, visited us in the ward. Standing next to the cot, he blessed our family. With his prayer, I felt a sense of ease. He was a gentle, giving man, his Sunday sermons were filled with compassion, and always uplifting. He received couples from hours away for marriage preparation and ceremony. I was shocked to learn that Catholic Protestant marriages were still frowned upon by some. The couples concerned had been rejected in their home parishes. They found acceptance and love with Jim. Sean's grandparents left New Ross, Wexford, in the 1900s because of this division. They were a Catholic

Protestant union. At the time, that was blasphemy. These divisions looked even more crazy in the face of the week we had passed through. What was more important than life?

With few doctors on site, given the holiday weekend, Mags said we could ignore the two-visitor limit so my mum could come with us the following day. The hospital rules were usually strict, so Mam had been home alone most days since Sophia's birth. It must have been lonely and difficult for her. On his way home, Jim stopped to see Mam, offered to collect her for the Easter Sunday service, and invited her to Sunday lunch with his family. It was like he had read my subconscious mind. He was a river of compassion.

There were fewer lines and tubes going into Sophia than in ICU. Only four remained, the feeding tube through her nose down into her stomach, a sedative line into a vein in her arm, the chest-drain, and a monitor attached to her chest. I changed her nappy for the first time. It made me notice her legs and feet. In ICU, I had focused on her delicate face, upper chest, and arms, where most of the tube action was. Now I realised her legs were long and her feet seemed big for her size.

My friend Brigid's baby Millie was born at 10.10 a.m. that day. She weighed more at birth than Sophia did at nine days. Unlike a normal baby, Sophia had been recovering rather than growing, she had lost weight, rather than gained weight, since birth. She wasn't moving, so her muscles weren't developing. For normal development she had to have the 'all clear' from the X-ray.

'Please God. Please heal Sophia's oesophagus fully. Please let there be no leaks.'

I prayed it again, and again, and again. Please God.

That evening I felt exhausted by the stress of not knowing. The milk didn't flow despite breathing into the blanket. I reminded myself to be thankful, but worry about the X-ray kept getting the upper hand.

I heard a car outside. Aideen was on the doorstep.

'I brought some fairy dust,' she said handing me a fairy book and a sparkly fairy doll for Sophia.

'Oh, Aideen. It's so good to see you. Thank you!' I hugged her and my eyes filled with tears. Since Sophia's birth I was like a garden sprayer, water constantly gushing down my face.

'Look at me. A weeping heap.'

'After what you've been through, you're allowed to be a weeping heap. But a thankful heap too. You're almost there. We're on the final straight. Sophia will be home in no time.'

Aideen was right. Sophia was healing. I had to focus on that, and not think about what ifs.

'How's the expressing going?' asked Aideen looking professorial.

'You're a genius. The blanket and photo worked amazingly well yesterday. Today I wasn't so good. I'm too worried about the X-ray. I can't stop thinking about it, and stress blocks the flow.'

'Then relax. Don't force yourself. And don't say 'I wasn't so good'. You were, and are, great. Just remember that. Every effort matters no matter how small the result. Look at how fast she's recovering. It's miraculous. Try again tonight but don't get up early. You need a break. Enjoy this moment of peace. When she gets home, she'll wake you, and there'll be little chance to rest.'

'I can't wait,' I said laughing through my tears.

Aideen was extraordinary. She had arrived just when I needed her, with just what I needed, fairy dust and words of wisdom.

Easter Monday, the big day for the X-ray, dawned raining and miserable. Sean and I drove into hospital pretending to be normal, but we were nervous. It was ten days since Sophia's surgery. D-Day. We were ready and keen to know but scared.

When Vivan came around, he bore disappointment.

'We have to wait until tomorrow,' he said.

I felt let down. The businesswoman in me took over. I started disputing, trying to negotiate a place.

'What about later today?' I asked.

'No, it's Easter Monday.'

'Then how about after hours? We're happy to pay for overtime,' I haggled.

'No. We're short of staff. X-ray is for emergencies only. We have to wait until tomorrow.'

He wouldn't budge. I had to be patient. Like Sophia's wait in my stomach, perhaps her healing needed one more day. I consoled myself with that important message. As my sister Foo often said, 'everything is unfolding as it should.'

Through that Easter Monday, Sophia started to have awake times like a normal baby. She would watch us with a bright face. Now that she was less encumbered, the nurses encouraged me to have her on my bare chest as much as possible. They called it 'kangaroo care'. All babies need it, but especially those in recovery. Like the milk, every moment on my bare skin was giving her the signal that she was loved, that she needed to get well, to live.

The day for the X-ray dawned again. This time the sun was shining bright and there was a brisk wind coming off the Irish sea. Sean and I held hands as we walked the beach wrapped in coats and scarves. We would never have guessed back on that sunny afternoon when we threw caution to the wind that we would go through the emotional roller coaster of the previous twelve days.

After our walk we were calm, it felt like the wind had cleared our minds and blown away our fears.

At Temple Street, Sophia had been off food for a couple of hours in preparation for the X-ray. The nurses disconnected her tubes and passed her to Sean. She was in good form despite hours with no food.

Mags explained how to get to the X-ray Department and sent us on our way. Walking down the corridor from the ward to X-ray was the first time we had been alone with our daughter. I felt like when we had a day out from boarding school. Freedom.

'Should we make a run for it?' asked Sean, sensing the same thing.

We laughed and laughed. Sophia's eyes followed me like a magnet.

We found our destination, quit our crazy laughing, went in, and waited patiently in the anteroom. The X-ray nurse opened the door, and I felt a rush of adrenalin like I was preparing for an exam.

'Sophia, for the oesophagus,' she said. 'I'm Rachel, I'll be doing the X-ray. Only one parent can come in.'

'You go in, Caro,' said Sean making to pass Sophia to me.

'Wait a minute, Dad,' said Rachel. 'We need to get the lead protection on Mum first. You can come in to get Sophia settled, but you need to leave before we do the X-ray.'

She opened the only cupboard in the room, took out a weighty grey suit and placed it over me.

'That's to protect you from the X-rays. Now I'll explain what we're going to do. I have a small bottle of liquid that Mum will feed to Sophia. As she drinks it, the liquid will highlight in the oesophagus, and we'll see if it passes from mouth to stomach with no problems. Clear?'

We both nodded. I understood the steps but inside I was a cauldron of nerves.

Rachel led us into the X-ray room and showed us where to place Sophia, then strapped her in. She looked so small on the examination table, but she was calm, watching us, wondering what was up, totally unaware of the critical moment taking place. Rachel passed a baby bottle to me.

'You'll see me through that window,' she said, pointing. 'I'll give a thumbs up as the go ahead. When I do, you start feeding Sophia the bottle.'

'What if she doesn't want to drink it?' I said.

'Oh, I think she will after having had nothing to drink for a few hours. And this is sweet. She will like it. Now Dad, if you could leave the room, we'll get on with it.'

Sean gave my hand a squeeze, walked out, and closed the door behind him. Rachel disappeared out of another door and reappeared at the window. The machinery above us whirred, then moved into position above Sophia. She was quiet, looking about, evaluating it all. I was less calm.

'Please God let there be no leaks.' I prayed it again and again.

Rachel gave the thumbs up, and I put the bottle into Sophia's mouth. She gripped on and started sucking. My heart raced; I looked up to the X-ray monitor on the wall. It showed the liquid going down her throat into her oesophagus through a wide part then a tight section then another wide part and into the stomach. It appeared to pass in a smooth motion despite slowing at the thin section.

The tight part was obviously where the connection was. To my untrained eye the liquid appeared to have passed through with no problems. I felt like yelling Hallelujah, tap dancing down the corridors, and shouting the news to everyone in the place. It was the first time Sophia had drunk anything normally in her life. My mind flashed back to the day of the operation as I watched her finish the last of the bottle.

The machine switched off, the monitor went blank, and Rachel came out beaming.

'Well, that's great news all together. Not a sign of a leak. The surgeon said it was a tight connection, but that didn't look tight to me. Congratulations, Sophia!'

'Thank you, Rachel,' I said, tears of joy running down my cheeks.

I opened the door to the waiting room. Sean was bent over, his forehead on his hands, praying. He looked up. I gave a thumbs up.

He leapt up and hugged me wide around the lead coat. Inside, Rachel was unstrapping Sophia. My body was a giant fizz of happiness as I said 'Thank you, God' ten times over as I watched her.

'Does this mean she's completely healed?' I asked when she looked up.

'For the moment, yes. Sometimes the connection, you saw it in the X-ray, doesn't widen and grow as it should, and a stent must be put in, but don't worry about that now. She's all clear and you should celebrate.'

I didn't know what a stent was, but I could guess. Anyway, I didn't want to dwell on that. I wanted to follow her instructions and break out the Champagne.

'Thank you, Rachel,' I said.

'You can pick her up now,' she said.

Sean took Sophia off the table. She was unaware of what a life-defining moment we had experienced, but she looked happy. Maybe it was the sugar water offering a momentary high.

We walked down the corridor, proud parents, our precious daughter reclining in Sean's arms, freed from the risk of more surgery. I felt like I was floating.

Sean looked over at me, his smile wide.

'Stop beaming like an eejit,' he said.

'I can't help it.'

We exchanged even wider beams, then laughed like two crazies. Sophia's eyes roved from one to the other, wondering what she had got herself into, hanging out with this pair of nuts.

Within minutes of returning to the ward, Vivan arrived.

'I looked at the X-rays. No leaks. We have the all-clear. Sophia's doing well on everything else too. I spoke with Prof. Puri, and we agreed that you can start breastfeeding this afternoon.'

I felt like jumping for joy.

'I need to take the chest drain out first. I'll be back after lunch to do that. If it goes well, you can start soon after that.'

Mary, a high-dependency ward nurse, who was at my side, joined the conversation.

'We have a room next to the ward reserved for you. Now that you're breastfeeding, you need to be nearby, so you can feed her every couple of hours.'

I was going to hold my baby and feed my baby like a normal mother. I could barely believe it. I felt the need to pinch myself to check I wasn't in a dream.

We called Mam and her communication centre went into overdrive. Thank yous and messages went out in waves to family and friends that had been praying for Sophia in South Africa, Canada, and beyond. Sophia had made it to the third milestone. She was healed.

Vivan could not come back fast enough for me. The arms on the clock above the nurse's counter moved ever so slowly. Lunch in the canteen was boiled cabbage, pork, and potatoes. It was solid, hearty, and, with my new status as a breastfeeding mum, free. For the foreseeable future this hospital would be my home and this canteen would be where I would eat so I was available to Sophia 24/7. As we were eating a practical detail hit me, I needed an overnight bag.

Mid-afternoon, while Sean collected my overnight bag packed by Mam, Vivan came back. He gave Sophia a local anaesthetic, then took out the chest drain, and sent us back to X-ray to check the drain area was all clear. This time Sophia hated it. Once she was strapped in, I had to hold her arms and legs down. She screamed blue murder. I saw it as a good sign. At least we knew she could let us know when things were not going well for her. Another tube was removed. Slowly Sophia was being liberated.

Back in the High Dependency Unit, Mary gave Sophia paracetamol for the pain. She kept crying. I was beside myself with worry. I tried holding her, but she seemed to get more aggravated.

'She's still in pain. Please give her some more painkiller,' I said to Mary.

'I can't. That's the maximum dose I can give her for now. We have to wait for it to take effect,' she replied. 'Babies cry.'

Not my baby. She had never cried like this. Sean returned. He lifted her from the cot, snuggled her, and started walking circuits round the ward. He had her calm within a few minutes and looking angelic for the arrival of Vivan and Dr Murphy, the paediatrician from Holles Street. Sean, Mary, and I gathered around to listen to their prognosis.

'You can start breastfeeding this afternoon,' said Dr Murphy. 'Well done for sticking with it.'

'Thanks Dr Murphy,' I said. 'It was my friend Aideen, she's a part time breastfeeding counsellor. Without her I wouldn't have thought of it or been able to make it happen.'

'Well, she's done a great service. Sophia has recovered remarkably well,' he said.

The look on his face was a look of satisfaction, like a mechanic saying to himself, 'That repair went well'. He had to do that. He couldn't become personally attached. His detachment was his way of staying sane in a job where not all repairs went well.

'Now we have to be sure that she's gaining weight and then we can send you home.'

'I'll do my best,' I said.

'She really is a beautiful baby, isn't she?' He remarked as he turned to leave.

Sean and I beamed with pride. Luckily Dr Murphy hadn't seen Sophia a half hour before. She was back to her serene self. I watched the paediatrician's tall, thin silhouette disappear down the corridor and felt a wave of gratitude and love for him and all the people that had contributed to Sophia's recovery.

Vivan's voice brought me back to the huddle around Sophia.

'Mary, I'll take the TAT out. After that, you can help Mrs Feely start breastfeeding.'

Mary scribbled dutifully onto her note board. It was like a classic cartoon scene of doctors round a hospital bed, and I felt like laughing. The relief of the day's events had made me lightheaded and a bit crazy.

While Mary, Sean, and I, held Sophia still, Vivan carefully removed the TAT (trans-anastomotic tube), a fine tube that had been posted through her nose, and down her throat, to transfer milk directly to her stomach. It was the last line to go. Sophia was free. There were no more drugs going in via a needle, the only pain relief now was a tiny dose of liquid paracetamol to ease the discomfort of the chest drain removal. Feeding from now on was breast or bottle, no more pockets of liquid down a tube.

I texted Aideen the good news and asked her to come as soon as she could. She replied she would come straight from work. She was my breastfeeding guru. Every new mum needed one. It was so exciting and thrilling, I felt on top of the world. Little did I know, real breastfeeding was going to be a serious challenge. It was natural. I expected it to be automatic. I was so wrong.

CHAPTER THIRTEEN

Boiled food and breastfeeding

Susan, the breastfeeding nurse at Temple Street, had been on call for us. She had heard the good news of the X-ray and knew it meant we would likely start breastfeeding that afternoon. She arrived within minutes of Mary's call. I reflected on the exceptional network of people this hospital had and felt a wave of gratitude.

Susan was a 'can do' person like many of the nurses we had met. True to her nature there was no messing. We got straight to it.

'We'll try a breastfeed now, shall we?' she said. 'Settle yourself comfortably in the chair there.'

I sat down and she passed Sophia to me and showed me how to hold her. I lifted my shirt and raised Sophia to the height of the nipple as Susan instructed. With Susan advising and Sean standing by we tried to get Sophia latched on. She was having none of it. Like me, she didn't know what to do. Not only that, her first experience of breastfeeding had been a very bad one, that ended in a long operation and many dark days of unconsciousness. Her instinct, that had been in force then, had been buried.

I felt like an idiot. I expected breastfeeding to be natural, that I would know what to do, but it was not so. The more I tried to latch her on to the breast, the more she fought against it. She became aggravated. I felt stressed.

'Why isn't it working?' I asked, frustrated and disappointed.

This was what I wanted so badly; that Sophia would be well enough to breastfeed. Now here we were, and it was a failure. When I was expressing, I imagined that real breastfeeding would be easy, instinctive. A distant ambulance siren screamed closer and came to rest on the road outside. Sophia began crying in earnest. Her tiny face turned red with upset.

'We'll take a break,' said Susan. 'Perhaps Sean could feed her a little milk from a cup so she's not so starving that she roars the place down. Don't give her a bottle. If they start on that, it's hard to get them onto the breast. I'll come back in an hour, and we'll try again.'

Sean paced the room trying to pacify mighty Sophia with milk in a cup. We were beginning to realise that she ruled our world. When she cried, she was the master of us all. Until her problem was solved, nothing else could be done. A few sips and many circuits later, Sean placed her tenderly into her cot and she slept, worn out with it all. She wasn't the only one. We slumped into chairs and watched her; eyes glazed over in emotional exhaustion. We would have to learn to live with crying and how to solve it. As Kathryn and Mary had said, babies cry.

Sophia was just waking when Susan returned. I sat in the feeding chair and tried Sophia on the opposite breast. The orientation made no difference. She fussed and would not latch on. We were moving her to a new position when Aideen arrived. She leaned down to kiss me on the cheek and embraced Sean. I introduced her to Susan.

'Well, I'll leave you to it,' said Susan.

'Thank you so much Susan,' I said.

'I'll check in on you tomorrow,' she said, then turned, and disappeared down the corridor.

Sophia watched the proceedings, looking curious, as if she was wondering who this new player in the milk wars was. Would she also force her to do things she didn't want to do? Aideen's bright red shoes and red coat offset her silver white hair. Her short cut always had one longer strand that was high-lighted with a touch of colour, red one month, purple the next. She went grey in her early twenties and made a feature of it instead of hiding it. She looked fantastic. Sophia's eyes followed Aideen, fascinated by the movement and the colour.

'At last!' she said, gently clapping her hands and swirling her red coat slightly. 'How's it going?'

'Not good,' I replied. 'She won't latch on. Neither of us knows what to do. Susan gave us the instructions, and tried to help, but it's been a struggle. A failing struggle.'

'Don't worry, that's normal. It's hard to do when you start, even in the best of circumstances.'

Aideen sat down beside me.

'Try squeezing a few drops of milk out so she gets the taste of it, then latch her on,' she said.

I changed direction, putting her back onto the left side, where I felt more confident being left-handed. We tried again. Sophia wasn't interested.

'Don't worry,' said Aideen. 'She's probably not hungry. She's had a heck of a day. She probably just wants to sleep. We'll try one more time. Try to relax. If you are stressed, she feels it.'

Aideen was right. She had had a heck of a day. She was fully conscious for the first time, feeling all the pain and joy there was to feel without serious painkillers. She had had two X-rays and crowds of people buzzing around her. No wonder she was feeling cranky.

As for me, learning to breastfeed with a relative stranger was not ideal. Susan's no-nonsense approach hadn't helped me to relax. I felt like I needed to perform, to make it work, rather than feeling a sensation of love and comfort as you should when breastfeeding. Sophia felt my angst and it made her worse. We were in a negative reinforcing circle of stress.

I took a couple of deep breaths. With my tight tribe of Sean and Aideen helping, I could relax. This was not a race. I settled back into the chair and lifted Sophia to the position Aideen had shown me, nestled on my left arm then squeezed a drop of milk out with my right hand. It hung there on the nipple, and I directed Sophia to it, holding her close. She latched on properly for the first time since her birth.

'Yippee!' said Aideen clapping her hands and doing two steps of an Irish dance. She and her daughter took dancing lessons with an octogenarian master dancer in Dun Laoghaire, she danced like a pro.

I felt on top of the world. We were breastfeeding. It felt so good, a deep satisfaction unlike anything I had felt before. Aideen leaned against the wall to watch us.

'Maybe a few supports will make it easier to relax, perhaps a cushion for under your arm, and a footstool. I'll bring them tomorrow.'

I watched Sophia in contentment. After a couple of minutes, she let go. I looked to Aideen for guidance.

'That's great. She's had enough for now. You have the position, and you know what to do. Now when she's hungry, everything will go well.'

I took a deep breath of Sophia's baby aroma and passed her to Sean. He walked around the ward a few times snuggling her then placed her delicately back into the cot. Watching him and our daughter, I felt a sense of peace. We would learn each parenting skill in its good time. Breastfeeding was like riding a bike. I had to be patient. Eventually it would be instinctive.

'Now you are breastfeeding, make sure you eat enough for the milk production,' said Aideen. 'I recommend macaroni cheese, roast chicken, mashed potatoes, ice cream.' She paused, then added, 'I suppose you had better eat some green things too.'

We laughed. Aideen was known for her hearty appetite for things meaty and solid. She wasn't a fan of vegetables, but Barry was such a great cook, he was bringing her round to them. Baby spinach leaves were only acceptable if hidden under mounds of peas, feta, and grilled pine-nuts. Aideen gave us both a hug, and disappeared in a swirl of cherry red.

Sean and I wandered down to the canteen for supper. As we took our trays and lined up along the self-service area, I waved to the anaesthetist that had taken care of Sophia. I didn't know if he was keeping track of Sophia's progress since she had moved on from his beat in ICU, but his wide smile seemed to say he did. I felt another wave of gratitude and warmth for the people that had saved Sophia's life, then turned to serve myself a large heap of mashed potatoes.

Sophia woke around 9 p.m. and I successfully latched her on again. She took a few good sucks then lost interest. Sean changed her nappy, walked circuits with her in his arms until she was asleep, then settled her back into the cot. He picked up his coat and book and kissed me goodnight. I felt lonely as I let go his hand.

'You had better get some sleep,' he said, then tiptoed out, pausing to wave goodbye from the ward door before his tall figure disappeared down the corridor and out into the cool night.

The ward was already in semi-darkness, a few low lights glowed around the nurses' counter. It felt serene and organised, like I imagined bedtime in an upper-class Victorian nursery. I picked up my book and whispered goodnight to the two nurses on duty.

'Sleep well,' said Maeve. 'I'll wake you when she calls for a feed.'

My tiny garret room was a few metres down the corridor. It was functional, a metal bed, a small side table and a closet. It reminded me of boarding school. I unpacked my toiletries bag and went down the corridor to brush my teeth and wash my face. Walking back, the sounds from the dimly lit hospital, the clatter of a nurse dropping something, a baby crying, a siren in the distance, reminded me not everyone was sleeping. I read a few pages, then tried to get to sleep. As I wondered if I ever would, I dozed off. A shake of my shoulder woke me at midnight.

'Sophia is hungry,' whispered Maeve.

Being woken in the middle of the night in strange circumstances I felt adrenalin burst through me. I leapt up, put on my gown and slippers, and followed her through to the ward. Theresa, the other night nurse, was pacing with Sophia, keeping her from waking the ward. I sped across the room wide awake and sat down in my feeding chair. Theresa passed Sophia to me. I pulled my nightie down and lifted Sophia to my right breast. She wouldn't have it, and no wonder. I was stressed, it was my first night in hospital, my first night breastfeeding. I felt panic rising. I reminded myself to go through the steps Aideen outlined, slowly and methodically.

'Ignore the pressure of waking the whole hospital,' I told myself. Easy to say. 'Concentrate on Sophia and the steps.' I took some deep breaths then tried again, calmly, and logically. This time Sophia latched on. I settled in, deeply content, but she stopped quickly, and conked out to sleep.

'We gave her fifty millilitres by cup at ten. Since you had just gone to bed, we didn't want to wake you,' said Maeve.

At 10 p.m. I was still awake having just put the light out after reading for fifteen minutes. I could easily have fed her, but they didn't know that.

'Thanks Maeve, but if she needs a feed, please wake me, even if I have just gone to bed. I need to get used to it,' I said.

'Okay, sure,' she replied, but I could see she was a little put out.

'I know you were doing what you thought was best, being kind to me, but when we're home, I'll have to get up, so I need to get into the habit,' I said, trying to ease the tension.

At four they woke me again. Sophia took up what was becoming a regular struggle at the start of each feed, she turned away and fussed. I tried to latch her on with the drop of milk trick, but she didn't fall for it. She groused. She fretted. She chewed on the nipple then turned away again as if in disgust. I felt like putting her back in the cot and asking the nurses to get the formula.

Maybe I wasn't made for breastfeeding. I wanted to do it, but I was failing. I was at my weakest point, lacking sleep, impatient to get back to bed, plus I didn't have Aideen, Susan, or Sean, on hand for help and advice. Despite my will to breastfeed and what I had said to Maeve, waking up through the night was difficult. I was new to this process as was Sophia. Fortunately, we were both stubborn. We kept trying.

At last Sophia latched on. Once she was feeding peacefully, my impatience to get back to bed disappeared and euphoria replaced it. She fed for ten minutes on my left breast. It was her longest feed so far. Aideen had told me to keep a diary of which breast and how long so I could track what was happening and knew which to start on the next time. She assured me that in time, it would be instinctive, but for now I had to work at it. After watching the struggle for a while, the nurses had wandered off. As I put Sophia back into the cot and prepared to change her, Maeve returned.

'You go to bed. We'll change her so you can get some sleep.'

'Thank you!' I said gratefully. I was becoming a 'normal' mother, but with two professionals helping me.

The pillow was hard. As I drifted off, I made a mental note to ask Sean to bring my pillow from home. We hoped it would only be a few days in the hospital, but we didn't know exactly how long. I could be on boiled vegetables and a boarding school bed for a little while yet.

It felt like minutes later when Niamh shook my shoulder gently and said, 'Sophia needs a feed.' The birds were singing a dawn chorus outside. Spring had arrived while we were in crisis. It was 6.45 a.m. I felt the joy of the morning and excitement for the day despite my lack of sleep, scratchy eyes. I was breastfeeding. Sophia was well.

Perhaps it was my mood, or perhaps it was getting familiar, or both. Whatever it was, Sophia latched on swiftly. A warm satisfied feeling swept through me. I nestled my tiny daughter against me and felt the glow that comes from breastfeeding, from the unique closeness that it provided. Her rosy cheeks and blue eyes looked up lovingly at me, and her baby smell engulfed my senses bringing with it a contraction of my uterus.

This satisfaction is called maternal fulfilment, something that is a key benefit for breastfeeding mums. It's a special feeling, something akin to being in love but deeper in its sensation, like eating a roast dinner compared to eating an oyster. It felt like partner love, but not as fizzy. There was more than maternal fulfilment to breastfeeding, it also helped the mother lose weight gained in pregnancy and delayed the return of a monthly period. There were benefits for me and for Sophia.

The smell of bacon and eggs wafted up from the kitchens and I began to think of breakfast. I tucked Sophia back into her cot and went downstairs. Taking Aideen's advice to eat well, I stacked my plate with fried eggs, bacon, black pudding, mushrooms, tomatoes, and fried potatoes, and breakfasted like a queen. Alone.

Staying away from my family was lonely, no matter how friendly the nurses and other staff were. They had their lives to live. When Sophia and I checked out, they would carry on here. For their sanity, they needed to keep their connections with patients and patients' families at a professional distance.

Back in the ward, lips greasy with breakfast, I pulled a chair beside Sophia's cot, and opened my book. I had barely read a page when the doctors' rounds started.

'Sophia is doing fantastically,' said Vivan. 'I know I have said it before, but I'll say it again, breastfed babies recover faster and withstand infection better.'

I wiped my hand over my lips hoping lingering grease wasn't giving away the extent of my breakfast. Sean would be jealous when I told him about it. Despite the quality of the canteen, I had one thing on my mind.

'When can we go home?'

'I can't say. We want to be sure that Sophia is gaining weight steadily before we send you home,' he replied.

'If I stay on eating breakfasts like I had this morning I'll be gaining weight even if Sophia isn't.'

'It's likely the other way around,' said Vivan. 'She'll gain weight and you'll lose weight because you are breakfasting, I mean breastfeeding.'

Mags, the nurse on duty, joined us in laughter.

By the time Sean arrived, my breasts were tender. By mid-afternoon my left breast had blisters and even with Sophia latched on correctly, I was in agony. Having a baby sucking on my nipple was very different to expressing by hand.

I had done a single day of breastfeeding and I was in bits. Sophia was feeding every three hours and the blisters got worse with each feed. It was so painful that I started to dread it. I called Susan and she promised to stop by to see me.

'Let's have a look, then,' she said. 'Hmm. Yes. Blisters. You're going to have to grin and bear it until they toughen up.'

'But Susan, it feels like a million needles are being stuck into my nipples when she sucks. This can't be normal.'

'You have sensitive skin Caro. You'll toughen up over time. If it's too awful, take paracetamol for the pain.'

I was stunned. I couldn't believe that this sort of pain would accompany something as natural as breastfeeding. That said, the birth of a baby was natural and accompanied by pain that defied description. Nonetheless there had to be something I could do rather than just grimacing and bearing it. After Susan left and Sophia was fed, I went out to call Aideen.

'You shouldn't be in agony. It should be a pleasurable experience, not torture,' said Aideen.

'What can I do?' I asked.

'You need to coat your nipples in lanolin. That'll be a protective barrier. Did Susan check your position?'

'No, I wasn't feeding when she popped in.'

'If Sophia is positioned incorrectly that could aggravate it, so we need to check that. It sounds like I should come in and see you, but I have the kids home on holiday. I can't leave them.'

'Maybe Sean can babysit so you can do a Florence Nightingale visit?'

Aideen laughed. An hour later Sean was watching over her son and daughter, and Aideen was flying over to me, fairy Godmother that she was. She arrived loaded with tubes of pure lanolin, a bright pink feeding cushion, and a footstool. She observed my technique. Sophia was a little reticent about my nipple now well covered in lanolin. Eventually hunger got the upper hand. Instead of a million needles I felt a couple of hundred. After checking that I had the 'baby in the crook of the arm', the most widely used position, perfect, Aideen showed me a few other holds. Breastfeeding was technical, my ideas about it coming naturally had been very wrong.

I started to make lists. Lists of different positions, lists of homeopathic solutions to breastfeeding problems, calendula for pain, belladonna for engorgement. With increased milk production, if a baby didn't drink as much as the day before, the breasts could became 'engorged'; too full. This could be eased by expressing, but it wasn't a good idea to over express or the problem would be worse the following day, as production would be further increased. Finding the balance in breastfeeding, as in life, was not easy.

Slowly the nurses handed responsibility over to me, transitioning me towards the day when we would go home. I was learning the ropes of being mother of a newborn at last.

I made a list of what to check when Sophia cried:

    1. Nappy?

    2. Ambient temperature: warm enough? Cool enough?

3. Bored?

4. Hungry?

5. Wind?

Over the following day, I successfully fed Sophia, my blistered nipples glistening with my new saviour, lanolin.

Mam came in to visit with Sean. It felt like a lifetime had passed since her visit a couple of days before. I had moved into the hospital and was becoming a mother. The nurses were teaching me and doing things that my mum would have done if we had been in a normal situation. I consoled myself that we would be home soon. Mam held Sophia for the first time, her first grandchild. I saw the special look on her face, that shows our hearts filling with love when we hold a newborn close. She had had to wait a long time, but we were finally there.

Sophia was getting the idea of day and night; she slept longer at night offering me a four-to-five-hour stretch and was more awake in the day. The night nurses, Niamh and Lorna gently woke me and offered a sense of humour and support in the dark quiet of the hospital night.

By day three of my hospital stay I felt like I was on a treadmill: feed Sophia, feed myself, sleep. The hearty boiled food gave me intermittent indigestion. I felt homesick.

Sophia gained 50g of weight and we said 'Hurrah!'

'If she gains consistently over the next two days, we can consider sending you home,' said Vivan.

Home was like a nirvana shimmering in the distance. Sophia had never been home.

Part 3: Home

'Home is a name, a word, it is a strong one; stronger than magician ever spoke, or spirit ever answered to, in the strongest conjuration.'

Charles Dickens

Chapter Fourteen

Parenting in the time of depression

'I hear you'll be heading home soon,' whispered Niamh. She was at my side as I cosied Sophia into my breast. The glow of the night light formed a halo around Niamh's dark hair.

'Yes, I hope so. I'll miss you all, but it will be good to go home,' I said.

'We'll miss you too. And the little dote, going home for the first time. That'll be something,' she said.

My focus shimmered with emotion. I had begun to root in this hospital, to feel part of it, and especially to know its people, doctors and nurses, canteen staff. The first of the kitchen's clatter started up. It was four thirty and breakfast was served from five.

'We might not see you tonight. I heard that you could even go home today if Sophia has gained weight.'

'Yes,' I whispered, feeling apprehensive despite longing for home. I was so fixated on going home, I hadn't considered that going home meant disconnecting from Temple Street. Home, something beyond a house, where we are with our family in the largest sense. Where we do not feel alien. I would miss this ancient hospital. When the night nurses left, we hugged affectionate goodbyes. I knew it was unlikely I would see them again and it felt strange given the intimate moments we had shared. There was something about the night that brought more closeness than the day. Their acts of kindness in the quiet hours of breastfeeding while the hospital around us slept, would stay with me forever.

Prof. Puri and the surgery team came through a couple of hours later. His rounds were so early that before I moved into the hospital, I hadn't seen him since the night of the operation. The Professor was happy with Sophia's progress. He gave us the thumbs up, the first of three deciders who needed to concur for us to leave. Next, we needed the agreement of the registrar, Vivan, and then the paediatrician, Dr Murphy.

'Hurrah!' said Vivan when he arrived, mimicking my hurrah the day before, and laughing. 'Sophia is on track with weight gain.'

'Hurrah!' I said lifting my arms in victory to match.

'You can go home today, but only after Dr Murphy's visit this afternoon. He should be here at around two, or a bit later. Sophia's been a model patient. Well done to you too, for pushing through with the breastfeeding.'

'Thanks, Vivan. I'm looking forward to going home, but I'll miss all of you.'

After Vivan left, I went to my room to pack up my clothes, toiletries, books, and pillow. Sophia was asleep when Sean arrived so we went down to the canteen for our last lunch; beef stew and mashed potatoes with boiled cabbage followed by sticky toffee pudding and ice-cream, the kind of food Aideen would approve of.

'To going home!' I said.

'To going home,' said Sean.

We clinked water glasses and our eyes met.

'Prof. Puri said the fastest home was two weeks. We're going home at two weeks and two days.'

Sixteen days before, we were praying that the surgery would be possible, that Sophia would make it through the life-saving intervention. It felt like a lifetime had passed. Memories washed over us. Seeing our daughter through surgery and recovery had been challenging. Having a child is testing for a couple, it pushes your relationship into a different space. We were at the start of our journey, but it felt like our relationship had been strengthened by our shared experience in this hospital and by having a child, like steel in fire. Now we were a family, the bond was stronger than when we were a couple. We were both responsible for our daughter, we would always be connected through her.

Back in the High Dependency Unit after lunch I felt sleepy, a nap would have been perfect, but I had quit my bedroom and given up the key. I fed Sophia and settled her into her cot, wishing I could snuggle in with her. Then we waited for Dr Murphy, desperate to get home and begin a normal life with our daughter. I dozed in the feeding chair and Sean read and paced. Mam was on stand-by at home, waiting. She had extended her stay so that she could help me for ten days after we got home. She couldn't stay away from my dad and her own home forever.

It was late afternoon by the time Dr Murphy and his cohorts arrived. Like other specialist doctors he was always accompanied by a team, an intern, and the registrar, at a minimum. I had Sophia nestled into my breast and she was feeding peacefully.

'That's a happy sight,' said Dr Murphy as he flicked through the charts. 'She's making good progress with weight gain. Well done, Mrs Feely. Yes, you can go home. Temple Street will book your appointments to see Professor Puri for surgery checks over the next couple of months. I'll see you for a general paediatric check at six months. You can book that with my secretary.'

He gave me his card and I carefully filed it in my wallet. Our eyes met for a moment.

'Is there any chance of a complication now? Is there anything we should watch out for?' I said.

'She's well on the way, there's little chance of a complication,' he said. 'Sometimes the connection constricts, and we have to put a stent in. If she starts vomiting regularly, call me.'

Before we could get to any emotional goodbyes, he turned and left, his thin figure disappearing down the hospital corridor. I thought back to the moment when he had announced Sophia's condition, how I had felt and what we had been through. I looked down at my baby breastfeeding and snuggled her even closer. A wave of gratitude and love swept through me.

'Come on, come on!' said Sean. 'She's just comfort sucking now. Let's go home!'

We would be driving into peak traffic, but we couldn't wait. Sean took baby Sophia, and I picked up my travel bag. We walked downstairs and out of the main door. We were Sophia's mum and dad, at last able to take on those roles in all their glory and responsibility.

At the car we debated how the baby seat should be attached to the seatbelt for so long that Sophia began to grouse. We were such newbie parents we didn't know how to attach it. Sean connected the car seat belt to the chair in what looked like the right places, then we belted Sophia into it. She looked so tiny and angelic. The first couple of kilometres were peaceful then Sophia started to give out. By O'Connell Street Bridge she was crying. By Ballsbridge, she was at full scream. I tried stroking her forehead, but it only made her madder.

'Do something!' shouted Sean. 'I can't drive with her screaming like that, I'll have an accident.'

I gave Sophia my baby finger and she sucked it in fury. By the time we got home my finger was numb. The instant I took it out of her mouth, so I could get out of the car, her little face crumpled. The familiar sounds of sea, birds singing, a DART train passing, mingled with the sounds of a baby crying. Mam was at the door.

'See if she's hungry, Toots,' said Mam. 'I'll put some tea on.'

We realised it was the nappy. It must have happened as we left Temple Street. Now her tiny bottom was red. I felt like an irresponsible parent. Sean changed her and slathered on a thick layer of Sudocrem, our new best friend. With her problem solved, Sophia was peaceful again. We drank tea with Mam and basked in the joy of being home. We took turns holding Sophia, ogling over how beautiful she was.

A wicker basket for newborns, leant to us by friends, was next to our bed. When it was time to settle Sophia for her nap before the final feed of the day, Sean rocked her in his arms then placed her into the basket. She appeared asleep, but each time he put her into it, she woke up and screamed like she was being tortured. She was on guard, she knew she was in a new place, and she needed to be alert. She didn't want to be left alone. Sean rocked her, until his arms were numb. When she was fast asleep, he transferred her carefully to the basket.

Later, when he set her down for the night, she played the same game. Sean kept comforting her until she was fast asleep, then placed her into the basket, taking extreme care not to make a sudden movement. That night, I woke at the slightest murmur and fed Sophia. Every couple of hours she needed feeding. She was unsettled and needed comfort.

Sean went to work, and Mam and I took on the first day. We held Sophia close, making up for lost time. It was great to be home and to have Mam with me, but Sophia wasn't happy. She cried and cried. We took her for walks, held her, fed her, changed her, loved her. Within minutes of solving one problem, she would start crying again. We were in perpetual motion.

When Sean came home, Sophia was peacefully asleep for what felt like the first time since he left that morning. Mam and I were slumped on the sofa, no dinner had been made, no washing had been done. We had survived. Sean started to talk, and we both reacted like we had been electrocuted.

'Sssshhhhhhh! Don't wake the mighty mite that just went to sleep,' I whispered.

It became her nickname, small but mighty, as she was. Sean began making dinner and despite his care, the 'mighty mite' was soon awake and crying. I felt like crying. I made an SOS call to Aideen and got Barry.

'Sophia won't stop crying, we've been through all the potential problems. She never did this in hospital. We don't know what to do.'

'She's probably feeling unsettled with the change. She needs comfort,' said Barry.

'We've been holding her a lot today, it helps for a while, then she starts crying again,' I said.

'Perhaps you should try a soother,' said Barry.

'I read they were a bad idea so we're trying to go without one,' I said.

'Cillian had one. He hasn't had any problems as a result,' said Barry. 'Juliette wasn't interested. Maybe Sophia will take to it, and it'll help.'

Barry was practical. I had worked with him in the technology multinational where he and Aideen worked. He had been instrumental in getting me the role on a project in Ireland after we had met on a training programme in Belgium. That project led to an offer to move permanently from South Africa to Ireland with the company. Barry was generally one of the quieter members of a team, but when he spoke, people listened. When he took charge, things got done. The 'no soother' nonsense I had read went out the window. I asked Sean to forget about cooking supper and go forth and procure a soother. He returned with two. As eager as a drug addict I unwrapped one, sterilised it and popped it into Sophia's mouth, wide open in an angry howl. She spat it out and carried on screaming. I tried again with a dash of milk on the soother. This time she gripped on and kept sucking.

I looked up at Mam and Sean with a hesitant grin. How long would the quiet last?

'Let's hope it works for long enough to finish making dinner,' said Sean and raced back into the kitchen.

'And eating it!' I called after him.

Mam and I watched Sophia, expecting her to spit the soother out, at any moment, but she kept sucking. Peace as last.

'Thank you, Barry!' I said and held my hands together to the sky in a gesture of namaste.

I left Mam to watch our Sophia Fury sucking the life out of the soother and dragged myself up the stairs for a bath laced with lavender oil. The calming oils from my 'birth plan' were coming into good use. It would take that, and more, to recover from the ravages of the first day at home.

⁕⁕⁕⁕⁕ ⁕⁕⁕⁕⁕

Even with the soother, the new home-based Sophia was not as calm as hospital Sophia. Perhaps it was the lack of painkillers, incompetent parents, change, or a combination of all of these. Whatever it was, I realised how much help the nurses had provided. There weren't enough hours in the day, even with Mam to help. The transition phase of staying in the hospital allowed me to learn the ropes of breastfeeding and baby basics from professional nurses, another major positive side effect of breastfeeding. If I had merely been visiting the hospital during Sophia's stay in the High Dependency Unit, instead of living there, the change to home would have been even more dramatic, and difficult, for her and me.

The days passed in a flurry of feeding, changing, washing, cuddling, and crying. We improved slowly, getting better at anticipating Sophia's needs, and understanding why she was crying.

She loved her first bath at home. Mam showed me how to hold her, how to grip her tiny body to keep her safe. Mam was such a natural, she did it so confidently. I felt ham-fisted, wondered if I would ever get the knack of mothering my baby.

Sean perfected his technique for putting Sophia down for the night. First, he walked circuits with her in his arms downstairs, Bruce Springsteen's 'Tunnel of Love' album on low. Once she was fast asleep, he carefully climbed the stairs. In the bedroom he rocked her for another five minutes to be sure she was deeply asleep, then placed her into the basket. It was as if the basket held an alarm for her. One false move, and she would wake up, and he would have to start the whole process again.

Once he was successful and she was down, we tiptoed around, whispering so as not to wake her. I dropped a pot and we stopped like rabbits in the lights, waiting for the wail. Then we giggled hysterically, but quietly, feeling euphoria at having escaped the danger, then laughed some more at how ridiculous it was that we were hostage to our tiny, but mighty, daughter. We learnt exactly which steps creaked and dutifully stepped over them. We tiptoed into our room and got into bed in total darkness and silence.

In the morning after Sean left for work, and Sophia was down for her morning sleep, Mam and I sat at the old pine table folding washing. Spring was turning to summer; the fig cutting was covered in dark green leaves like large thick fingered green hands. A few figs were starting to form.

'I'm going to miss you Mam,' I said. 'How will I cope without you?'

'You'll be fine, Toots,' said Mam, reaching over to squeeze my hand. 'You're a pro at the breastfeeding now. Sophia's settling down. You're ready.'

'I don't know. I feel nervous about it. I don't feel like a confident mother. I don't feel competent, confident or in control, and I hate that.'

I was used to being on top of things, I was a bit of an A-type personality, I strove for success, and liked to feel like I was winning. I didn't feel like I was winning on the mothering.

'You are in control. Babies love a routine. You have to get one in place, then keep adjusting as they grow.'

'What you're saying is just when I've got the routine down pat, she's going to change it?' I burst out laughing.

'Yes,' said Mam joining me in the laughter. 'That's what babies do. They change every day. But don't worry. You're going to be fine, Toots.'

That afternoon, Sophia wouldn't settle after her feed. I was at my wit's end.

'Let's get her into the buggy and go down to the sea. That should help,' said Mam as she finished washing up our lunch dishes.

Sophia glared at us over an open roar as we strapped her in. From the angry look, she moved to the suspicious 'what are you monsters planning to do with me now?' look, while keeping up the howl.

We took off down the path, me checking side to side for neighbours. They would wonder what sort of torture we aliens inflicted on our young. But by that time, I was no longer officially an alien. I had applied for, and received, my Irish passport based on having lived in Ireland for five years and being married to an Irish citizen.

As we passed Annetta's house, the last on the path to the sea, Sophia stopped crying. She looked about curiously. I could picture a bubble over her head thinking 'Ha ha, got you! All the neighbours will think you're an evil mom-lady.'

'Evil mom-lady' was a term from 'Calvin and Hobbes' cartoons by Bill Watterson, that Sean used for me when Sophia was giving extreme dissatisfaction signals. By the end of the hardcore sea-path, where we turned to head back, she was fast asleep.

'You see Mam. How will I cope without you? You knew exactly what to do.'

'And now you know,' said Mam. 'You'll be fine. And you have amazing people like Aideen and Annetta nearby if you need help. Sean is just a call away when he's at work.'

'You're right,' I said as we lifted the buggy into the house, careful not to wake sleeping Sophia. 'Thanks Mam. I'm really going to miss you.'

I gave Mam a hug.

The motion in the buggy and the sound of the sea put Sophia to sleep. Even at her most upset it usually worked. But when Mam left, I felt alone and uncertain. Each time Sophia spat up a bit of milk my heart raced, adrenalin spiked, and I prepared for post-surgery complications. I knew the spits weren't serious, there was no vomiting, but I couldn't help my reaction. At night I woke at the slightest murmur. We underestimated how much post-traumatic stress Sophia and I had.

Breastfeeding became easier with practice, but if I had the slightest mistaken latch, blisters formed. Lanolin was my saviour. I smelt like a sheep and felt like a cow. My breasts developed lumps that were red and painful. I self-diagnosed blocked ducts. To solve the problem, massage and heat before breastfeeding, and a cold compress and rest after, were recommended. Blocked ducts were attributed to fatigue and stress. They could be a pre-cursor to a wholly more serious thing, mastitis, which required antibiotics. I attacked the problem as a project manager does, laying out the heating, massaging, and cooling, in a regimented programme. I felt like a pervert sitting alone on the sofa massaging my breasts.

Breastfeeding is an art. Despite the difficulties, I knew it was best for the health of my daughter, and for me. Sophia and I went to a local breastfeeding group in the hope of finding support; but I didn't feel at ease. The members were all stay at home mums, many on their second, third, or even fourth baby. I felt out of place.

I wasn't getting enough sleep and I felt like I didn't trust myself fully with Sophia, like I didn't really know how to care for her. When Sean was home it felt safer. When I was alone, I felt like I would go mad when she wouldn't stop crying. She was unpredictable. One afternoon everything would be perfect, and the next afternoon, I'd follow the same routine, and wind up with her screaming the house down.

One day, I called Sean in total state. He told me to put Sophia safely in her cot, lock the house and go for a walk. It would do her no harm and it would save me. I stepped it out to the end of the road and then ran back, worried and guilty for having left her. Sophia was fast asleep. I was relieved but embarrassed at my action.

The blocked ducts were not co-operating despite my well laid programme. Aideen popped in to visit and I burst into tears.

'I'm not coping. Maybe I'm not made for breastfeeding,' I said, wiping my eyes, then my nose.

'It's normal that you're exhausted,' said Aideen. She hugged me. 'People blame breastfeeding, but it's the stress of being a new mum that's behind how you're feeling. If you weren't breastfeeding, it would probably be worse. You had to stay strong while Sophia was at risk, now your system's demanding attention.'

I felt like Seneca more than two thousand years before.

'What need is there to weep over parts of life? The whole calls for tears.'

And he hadn't even had a baby.

I wasn't prepared for the emotional roller coaster I was on. None of the prenatal classes had gone into postnatal depression. They had brushed over it in passing. Despite modern medicine, childbirth is traumatic, and the shock, and wonder, of becoming a parent, turns life upside down. When depressive hormones are added, it becomes a toxic cocktail. Add to that the trauma we had experienced, and you have a dangerous mix.

Aideen was my lifeline. She provided stoic advice and called regularly to check on me and offer support. I focused on surviving one day at a time. When Sophia was asleep, I forced myself to do chores, but sometimes, I lay on the sofa, weeping, exhausted, a hormonal wreck.

One evening Sean found me in a puddle of tears.

'Maybe I wasn't meant to be a mother, perhaps it's all a terrible mistake,' I said, rubbing my sleeve across my face.

Sean passed me a tissue. He tried to console me, but I cried even harder. He called Mam and brought the phone to me.

'I'm so sorry, Toots. Oh darling, I wish I was there to help you,' said Mam.

I dissolved into fresh sobs.

'I know this doesn't help how you feel right now, but you mustn't worry,' said Mam. 'How you're feeling is totally normal. You're sleep deprived and experiencing postnatal depression. Many new mums get it, and with the stress of Sophia's arrival, you've probably got a double dose.'

'But what am I going to do Mam? How am I going to look after my daughter if I can't even look after myself?'

'Give yourself a break. Take paracetamol and try to get some sleep now that Sean's home,' said Mam.

'But I can't sleep. I'm so tired, but I can't sleep,' I said, sobbing harder.

'Then have a lavender bath and relax. Don't add any more pressure than you already have. If you can't sleep, just rest. I promise it's just a phase. You have to look after yourself and rest.'

'Thanks Mam,' I said, starting the hiccupping stutter that always came with lots of crying.

'You must look after yourself, Toots,' she said emphatically. 'Go for a walk on the beach every day. Wrap Sophia up in the buggy and go. You know how she loves it.'

She was right. Sophia did love it. She loved the motion and the sound of the sea. Sometimes it was the only way to quiet her. I had been feeling so down I hadn't done it for a couple of days. It would help me sleep better if I got out for a walk.

I nodded and made a strange yes that sounded like a long 'Hmmm,' followed by another gasping sob.

'You need to get exercise, Toots, that will help you feel better, and sleep better. When Sean gets home go for a quick run,' said Mam.

I knew Mam was right. All these things were true. I had no experience looking after a baby, I was the youngest in our family and never had to look after siblings. I also didn't have an extended family to rally round. Thank God I had Aideen.

'Are you eating properly?' asked Mam. She was on a roll, there was no stopping her now. 'When you're breastfeeding, you need to keep your strength up.'

'Maybe not enough,' I said. I hadn't even had time to eat properly.

Perhaps lack of calories was also contributing. After saying a tearful goodbye, and promising to take her advice, I went downstairs and ate a large bowl of ice cream and chocolate sauce. Mam had made four jars before she left, so I would be well supplied.

One bowl a day clearly wasn't enough. I made it my mission to eat two bowls, one after lunch and one late afternoon. I was eating more than I had ever eaten in my life, but I wasn't gaining any weight, in fact, I was losing it. It made me even more determined to stick with the breastfeeding. Two bowls a day of my favourite dessert was good encouragement.

Our friend Penny, that we met in the Alien's queue, experienced deep postnatal, also called postpartum, depression. Andrew was a pilot, so he was away from home a lot. Over the first few months of motherhood, Penny struggled with depression and learning to be a mum, with limited support. At the time I didn't register Penny's distress. I had never experienced it myself. It was only years later that I realised how bad it had been.

Postnatal depression is extremely serious and the antenatal, and postnatal, care I experienced didn't give it much attention. In addition, the modern world, super connected electronically, but often disconnected humanly, in terms of neighbours and family living nearby, can compound the loneliness a first-time mum feels.

I called Jacky, our pharmacist, to ask for sleeping pills that I could take while breastfeeding. She recommended a homeopathic lifesaver. Her pharmacy was conveniently located on the road between our house and Aideen's, so it was a good excuse to visit her.

At the time, I felt so overwhelmed by everything that needed to be done for my daughter, that I couldn't imagine going out for leisure. When I saw people with newborns, out for a leisurely lunch, or doing non-essential shopping, I would stare at them in disbelief. How did they do that?

Leaving the house for fun was beyond my comprehension, but for sleeping tablets, I would brave it. I checked I had everything in the bag, soother, wipes, nappies, sudocrem, a bag of raisins for me. We set off. Sophia watched me suspiciously as I attached the seat then buckled her in. Once we were on the move, I kept checking her in the rear-view mirror. I felt like a rebel as we made our way from Killiney to Monkstown Road.

At the pharmacy I parked right up near the door so I could see her from inside. I was too scared to undo the chair in case I couldn't get it attached again. I told Sophia what I was doing, made sure she had her soother, and locked the car. I got the goods from Jacky and ran back to the getaway car. My trusty partner Sophia was still there. She looked relaxed and happy. I leapt in. Minutes later we arrived at Aideen's. We were intact. Sophia wasn't crying, if anything, she looked intrigued with the new vistas.

Aideen instilled peacefulness. She sat me on the sofa, with some cushions for comfort so I could feed Sophia while she made us tea.

'There now. So, tell me how it's going?' she asked as she settled in beside me.

'We made it to the pharmacy, and then to your house,' I said. 'I feel like we climbed Everest.'

'Hurrah!' said Aideen, clapping.

'I need to get out more, but I don't feel ready for normal life yet,' I said.

'You're doing great. There's no rush. But if you do want to get out in a safe environment for new mums, my friend Nicola is hosting a support group for breastfeeding mums. I'll be going.'

'Thanks Aideen, that sounds perfect,' I said.

We left Aideen's house filled with tea and biscuits, a warm feeling, and a date in the diary. I had to get out and get back into life rather than moping at home. On the breastfeeding meeting day, I packed a bag with gear, nappies, changing equipment, and an all-important backup soother, and installed the car seat. Sophia was almost two months old, and I had only been out alone with her a couple of times. It felt edgy. Going to Aideen was one thing, striking out across the city was another. I double checked that I had everything, then did a feed before leaving to be safe. It was only twenty-five minutes' drive, but it would be the furthest we had driven alone together.

In the car Sophia was quiet, the movement calmed her. It was all going so well. As we made the final turn, she started to cry. By the time I got her car seat that doubled as a baby carrier out, she was screaming. I walked in the front door and felt flustered. Sophia was crying so furiously I couldn't hear, or take in, any names, as I was introduced to the group gathered in the kitchen. I tried popping her soother into her mouth. She spat it out in disgust and cried even louder. I took her to the empty lounge and placed her carry car seat beside the sofa to check the usual suspects. Everything looked okay, but Sophia wouldn't stop. I felt overwhelmed. Nicola, the hostess, a breastfeeding counsellor, and professional nurse, came through to join me. She had heard about Sophia's rough start.

'The poor little dote,' she said. 'I think she's stressed. Perhaps a little massage will help. May I?'

'Absolutely,' I said, ready to try anything to calm my daughter.

Nicola sat down on a footstool and undid the foot of Sophia's Babygro, talking calmly to her all the time. She gently massaged one foot.

Sophia looked intrigued but continued crying for a few seconds, then she stopped crying, and began to gaze at Nicola like she was an angel, adoration radiating from her tiny face. Nicola moved to the second foot.

'She's beautiful,' said Nicola. 'After her tough start, she needs help to relax. The operation, the medicines, anaesthetics, antibiotics, the hospital, they all take their toll.'

As Nicola massaged Sophia's tiny feet, we chatted about Sophia's operation and her hospital experience, and mine, as a breastfeeding mum. Sophia was transfixed. Her gaze didn't leave her masseuse; perhaps to make sure she didn't abandon her with the 'evil mom lady'.

After the ten-minute miracle foot massage Sophia was calmer than she had been in weeks. Nicola showed me how to massage her feet. Tea and biscuits were served. Sophia remained calm. I chatted to people like a normal human being. These ladies could talk about babies but also a lot more. There was life after birth. Aideen was, once again, my saviour. On my return I added two more things to my checklist for what could be making Sophia cry; did she need her soother? Did she need a foot massage?

Sophia and I were on the road to recovery, physically for Sophia, and psychologically for both of us. I was discovering that recovery included far more than the healing of wounds. The spirit and soul also needed healing. Nicola's massage had shown me that my baby's discomfort wasn't only about basic needs. Sophia and I both needed love and support. We leaned hard on the third member of our family, Sean, who was facing his own challenges, with imminent chartered financial analyst exams.

Chapter Fifteen

The reality of motherhood

The room that had been Mam's bedroom, returned to being a study. Sean was back at work full time and in the last lap of preparation for his CFA finals. Our weeks of hospital vigil had put his study schedule back significantly. He had to catch up on lost study time with a baby girl that was recovering from trauma, and a depressed postnatal wife.

In those days less than ten percent of those who started the CFA finished it successfully. After nearly three years of effort, it was not the time to give up, despite our rocky start to parenthood. On weekends and at night, Sean would sit for hours with Sophia swaddled in his arms, focused on his books. Both would get a blissful look on their faces. Sean was like a male version of Madonna, and child. He was gentle and kind. I wrote a caption under a photo of the two of them at that time, 'the rarely sighted 'sleeping Sophia' and the oft-sighted 'exhausted Dad'.

We knew the signs of discontent. A small frown would form, then her bottom lip would stick out. From the lip signal we had about three seconds to solve the problem. We became master detectives, able to divine a nappy situation a single sniff, the need for food from a hungry look, or the need for sleep from a rub of the eyes. If Sophia was inconsolable at night, Sean would take her for a drive to get her to sleep. It had the same effect as the buggy. Now, I shudder to think of the pollution, the climate devasting CO_2, pouring into the air, in that innocent act. Global warming was something we didn't hear much about. The danger, and the need to stop fossil fuels, had been buried by fossil fuel lobbies.

My night life was hectic. I got up in the dark, fed my baby, changed her, went back to bed, got up, fed, went back to bed, got up, fed... You get the picture. One night making my way to the toilet after feeding, I kicked my toe on the door in the dark. I hopped instead of yelping, not wanting to wake Sean, or agitate Sophia, and lost control of my still slightly renegade bladder. In France women receive state funded sessions for 're-education' of their perineal muscles after birth. The sessions were to save you from what I experienced, or worse, the same effect, in public, after a sneeze or a cough. Re-education also improves your sex life. Not that I was thinking about that yet, although it might have lifted my spirits. A nurse had recommended perineal exercises in a postnatal follow up, but instruction ended there. I did the odd 'tighten relax' of the area, about three a day, after the lunch time feed, if I remembered, just so I could say yes, when the nurse asked.

Yes, everything was under control. Ha ha.

We hunkered down, Sean with his CFA, and me with learning the ropes of being a mum.

By Sophia's ten-week birthday, I was confident with breastfeeding, but our nights were still disrupted. She woke every few hours to feed. We moved her into a full-size cot in her own bedroom, but I still woke at the slightest murmur. Between breastfeeds, nappy changes, and bowls of ice-cream, I often walked the beach.

I'd organise to meet Annetta, or we'd bump into each other. We'd chat as her son played at the water's edge and the two babies slept. We swapped baby tips, mostly her to me, given her experience. We were not deep mothering types. Mostly, our conversation went off into other spheres, like feminism or environment. Like me, she worked in a male dominated world.

'Would you like to come in for some tea?' asked Annetta, one day after our walk.

'I'd love to,' I replied.

We knocked the sand off our shoes and Annetta helped me lift Sophia's buggy inside. We took our shoes off in the entrance area. Annetta's house was familiar yet different. The design was almost identical to ours, but her kitchen was open plan to the dining area and separated from the lounge by double doors.

Annetta turned on the kettle. Her son brought a puzzle to the table. His bright eyes looked up for recognition, as he quickly organised the pieces to fit together. I clapped. He fetched another.

'Would you like some grapes?' asked Annetta.

'Thanks, Annetta,' I replied.

She washed a bunch and passed the plate over to me. In the garden, birds were singing, the sun was shining. The walk to the sea had worked its usual magic, putting the babies to sleep, and making me feel good, despite another broken night. I took a grape.

'They taste so good,' I said.

'But not organic,' said Annetta. 'Organic often isn't available in the local shops.'

'I know. We used to go to the Saturday organic market in the city centre, but since Sophia arrived, we don't have time for that,' I said.

'Of course,' replied Annetta. 'Between work and kids there's not much time left.'

'On Saturdays I'd often wander into the city centre to have my hair cut, drink a cappuccino at a café or browse for a new book,' I said.

'Ah the life,' responded Annetta. Like me, she loved reading.

'Books and coffee. Pure heaven,' I said. I had started to appreciate coffee again. 'Before my handbag contained lipstick, money, and a phone with messages from friends on it... Now my bag's stuffed with eco-friendly wipes, nappies, and a phone that calls Sean.'

Annetta laughed.

'I only go shopping for essentials, and race round to finish in time for Sophia's next feed or sleep. I grab whatever looks vaguely like what I have on my list. There's no time to look closely at labels or read the fine print. That said, I should make time to read the fine print.'

I paused for a moment feeling a sudden stab of anxiety in my belly.

'I can't help but wonder what made the oesophageal atresia happen. I mean, I know the doctors say they don't know why. But I wonder if it was the plastic on the ready meals we ate, or pesticides in the non-organic food we ate or the non-organic wine we drank.'

'You can't blame yourself for it,' said Annetta. 'As the doctors say, no one knows. For sure, eating fresh food rather than ready meals is better for us.'

'You're good with that,' I said. There were bowls of fresh fruit and vegetables on the counter.

'I try to make dinner from scratch most days,' she said. 'It's time consuming but I think it's worth it.'

'But I wonder about the quality of fresh produce, even if it isn't processed,' I replied. 'I read that the systemic pesticides used in modern farming can cause cancer, nervous system disruption, and hormonal and genetic disruption.'

'Unless you grew it yourself or know the farmer it's hard to know exactly what's in it,' said Annetta. 'For us city dwellers that's not easy. On the face of it, organic is better since systemic pesticides are not allowed. But can we be sure that it's really organic?'

'I thought the EU had rules about labelling and certification so we can be certain,' I said.

'There are rules. But are they controlled properly?' said Annetta. 'It's a question. I don't know. Then there's the availability of organic. It's hard to find and it's expensive.'

'Except for baby food, there are lots of jars of organic baby food on the supermarket shelves,' I said.

'That's true. But isn't it better to have a fresh mashed banana rather than a banana from a jar?' asked Annetta. 'Think of the waste implications.'

'You're right. It's a minefield. I'm not sure my foggy brain can deal with this,' I said and laughed. Pregnancy, and early days of motherhood, bring a change in hormones that lead to what is sometimes called foggy brain, baby brain, or 'momnesia'. Shopping for a family wasn't simple. My brain felt like it couldn't compute navigating healthy food options and waste implications given my time and budget constraints. It was too much for me. Just getting through the day without landing in a weeping heap, was enough.

'Speaking of food, I'd better get home before the next round starts for Sophia. With my regime for the blocked ducts, it's better if I'm at home.'

Annetta burst out laughing, imagining the impact on her neighbours if I was seen following the 'anti-mastitis programme' I had described on our walk while sitting on her sofa.

'I suppose so,' she said, still laughing.

Back at home Sophia was an angel. She fed peacefully, looking adoringly up at me. Things were getting easier, but we were far from normal first-time parents. We were on alert and danger sensitive. That weekend, Sophia smiled at us for the first time, and we were even more smitten.

Brigid and her husband, Senan, visited with their daughters Pippa, and Millie, who was born soon after Sophia. We took a walk to the sea, then sat in the lounge to chat over tea. Brigid was a natural mother. I watched in awe as she handled a toddler and a baby, with no fuss. Entertaining them came naturally thanks to her skills in theatre, art, and music.

Senan, meanwhile, lived at speed. He had made it through four near death experiences. As a child, one of his brothers shot him through the eye by mistake. As a student, he was swept under a bus riding his bike. Then he was stabbed in the chest trying to stop a robbery.

The closest shave was in a Philadelphia hospital where he was pronounced dead on arrival after an intense asthma attack. They shocked him back to life. He was a journalist with a great passion for the Titanic and the history, and mystery, surrounding it, so much so, that he had written several books about it. Since meeting Brigid, he had had no near-death experiences, and had created life in his beautiful daughters. But sitting down for tea wasn't his style. He got fidgety.

To ease his fidgets, he picked up Millie and threw her into the air. I felt an instinctive need to leap forward to catch her, but held back, registering the shock internally. Sean and I watched wide-eyed, barely able to believe what we were seeing. Senan, oblivious to our horror, threw their baby again, and again. Millie laughed. I tried to still my racing heart.

We treated our Sophia with kid gloves, there was no throwing around for us, and no wonder. We couldn't see inside to know if she was fully healed but there was no unusual vomiting. Still, I was relieved when the surgery check-up with Prof. Puri rolled around. The faint whiff of overcooked vegetables and chlorine floating on the air brought memories of the weeks at the hospital flooding back. I felt remarkably serene. Everything was okay. Everything was going to be okay. The trauma we had experienced was slowly fading.

Prof. Puri checked Sophia's scars, then felt around her abdomen. I expected her to break into the signal for extreme dissatisfaction at any moment, but she behaved like a saint, perhaps she recognised her guardian angel. Everything was progressing in the best possible way. He asked if I was still breastfeeding, congratulated me on it, and made the point that it had contributed to Sophia's swift recovery.

I also knew it was thanks to the top neonatal surgeon in the world. Prof. Puri had written the neonatal surgery textbook used by specialist surgeons around the world. As the ICU nurse said on that first shocking day, he was the best of the best. There was no better city for our daughter to have been born with her special circumstances.

That day, I felt so confident and at ease traveling with Sophia, that I stopped into my office to introduce her to my colleagues. I parked the car, walked to the office and up the stairs to the top floor, carrying my precious cargo like a professional. I hadn't been into the office in months, my life had been focused on the life in my arms. I was a different person.

The creaking floorboards announced my arrival. Heads looked up from desks. Lorraine, our office manager, rose instantly, eager to hold Sophia. She didn't have children yet, but she was a nurturing person, made for mothering. The rest followed. Most of those without kids hung back, probably too frightened to hold her, like I had been too frightened to hold a baby before Aideen encouraged me on my first weekend in Dublin.

'Would you look at her,' said Frank, in his mild Cork accent. 'You'd never know she had been through all that.'

'She's beautiful. Sure, with Caro and Sean as parents, you wouldn't expect it,' teased another.

Seeing my friends and colleagues felt good. In minutes they had me laughing out loud and Sophia enchanted at the flurry of attention. I didn't stay long. The working day had to continue, and I had to keep to my Sophia regimen. Seeing them that day was good for me. I felt like I would be ready to go back to work in a few weeks when my maternity leave ended.

Leaving Dublin city that afternoon was a turning point. Sophia and I were in a happier place. I had transitioned from a weeping heap when Sophia was around a month old, to a tentative mom that set off to Nicola's massage parlour, to a confident mom taking Sophia to her appointment and to meet my colleagues. 'Baby Mothering 101' had been successfully completed. Back at the car, I placed Sophia into her car seat and attached it confidently, then tucked a light blanket around her. She gave me a smile. She felt it too.

A woman's hormones take about eighteen months to return to normal after having a baby. The chemical used to speed up the birthing process, and that I wanted turned off back in the birthing ward, oxytocin, is a powerful bonding chemical that makes us feel sensual and close to our partners. When a woman has a baby, that bonding chemical, focuses the mother's attention on the child rather than their partner. It can distance their partner as they attach themselves to their new child.

If a woman is breastfeeding, this disconnection can seem greater since they are the only one that can feed the baby. The partner can't offer a bottle and the mother can't leave her baby for longer than the time between feeds. Expressed breast milk in the freezer is a way around this. I got organised. Pockets of frozen milk meant I could get out for longer than two hours. They spelt freedom. It was good for me and for Sean. He strengthened his bond with his daughter, and I started running again.

My first run, I took the familiar path to the sea that was an almost daily pilgrimage for me and Sophia. Where the concrete ended, I joined a sandy track, wild grass like beige-green porcupines either side. Killiney beach stretched out ahead of me, views all the way to Sorrento Terrace and Dalkey Island beyond it. From the track I crossed a section of beach, uneasy on the pebbles, then through the tunnel that connected to the road at the DART station.

The route took me up the hill Sean and I had taken on the bikes the day we met kayak Rob. Breathing the iodine air, I felt magnificently alive. Near the top of Vico Road, the views were a good excuse to stop and walk. Above White Rock Beach I sat on the wall to catch my breath. The sea shimmered across Killiney Bay. Beyond our housing complex, Sugar Loaf peaked up, and Bray Head beyond it. Summer had arrived, dandelions set seed heads alongside flowering white clover. A butterfly flew up and danced across the path pirouetting back and forth before landing on a bramble, delicate lilac, pink, and white flowers, promising lush purple berries in my future. The endorphins, the loose-limbed joy of running, the views, the sea air, knowing Sophia was safely home, I felt like I would explode with happiness.

It was like a drug. I loved that run so much that I took it a couple of times a week. Sometimes, if the tide was super low, I stayed on the beach for longer and went up at White Rock. One day I followed the steps all the way up Killiney Hill. I stopped to stroke the bark of an oak tree, rough scales in uneven hoary patterns, against my hands, gaps wide enough for my fingers to slip into. I leaned on it for a moment, embarrassed to be seen hugging it, but wanting to. I pressed in pretending I was stretching.

I felt a connection, a sense of interbeing, like I was part of something bigger, a sense of sacredness. We are connected to trees and plants. They 'breathe' out oxygen that we breathe in and depend on. We breathe out carbon dioxide that they 'breathe' in and depend on, to perform their miracle of photosynthesis. They provide our food, or food for our food. We are all connected in the extraordinary web of life.

Later, as an organic farmer, I would learn about the magic of trees, their ability to communicate with each other, to support each other. Books like 'The Hidden Life of Trees: What They Feel, How They Communicate: Discoveries from a Secret World' by Peter Wohlleben, 'Finding the Mother Tree: Uncovering the Wisdom and Intelligence of the Forest' by Suzanne Simard, and 'Untangled' by Merlin Sheldrake, offered glimpses into the tree world, and the soil life that supported it.

Oak trees live for hundreds of years. Some of them connect us to a time long before the Anthropocene. The oldest oak in the world is thought to be around two thousand years old. Imagine that when you plant an oak today, it could still be here in the year 4000. Thinking twenty years out is hard, but 2000. One thing we can be fairly sure of is that the earth will still be here, flying through the cosmos.

Sometimes I didn't have the energy to run, and my outing would become a beach walk instead. I didn't take the time to sit on the beach and meditate on the waves. If I had realised how important it was to rest, to restore, to meditate, I would have been happier, and able to be a better mother.

Despite the check-up showing all was well, each time Sophia woke up crying, my heart raced, and adrenalin pumped. My stress made her stressed and stopped her from having a relaxed sleeping rhythm. At three months, babies should sleep for a stretch of at least six hours at night. We were still up every three hours. To survive I needed an afternoon nap when Sophia took hers. I wondered how I would cope when I returned to work and couldn't take one.

A month later, when I went back at work, we took to the new morning routine of getting ourselves and our four-month-old ready for the day, remarkably easily. We started a mantra 'Don't forget your dodie if you want to go to crèche', following the cadence of Christy Moore's 'Don't forget your shovel if you want to go to work'. In Ireland, a soother is called a dodie, and Sophia was still very attached to hers. Forgetting a dodie was a serious crime. I bought a backup and left it in the car.

The crèche required parents to collect their children by 6 p.m. Fines and bad karma were imposed on the guilty. Dublin traffic was a nightmare at that time of the evening. Previously I arrived to work early and often left late. Now I changed my work schedule to arrive early and leave early. Sophia and I were out of the city by 4 p.m. That moment of collection was bliss, I loved this small human with a force beyond understanding. The need to be with her was like a powerful magnet, a physical force. My work colleagues were supportive. Frank's wife Suzanne, had had a baby two months after Sophia. They were learning the ropes like we were. He understood.

Sean passed his CFA with flying colours. He took a second job teaching night classes for the Master of Finance students at National College of Ireland. We had a vague dream to move to France. For that to become a reality, we needed money. We juggled our new parenting life into our work lives.

While I rejoiced in being back at work and back to a more 'normal' life, Sophia not sleeping through was taking its toll. We procured a book that promised to solve our problems. The author declared that we had to leave the baby to cry to teach them to self-comfort so they would get to sleep, and back to sleep, on their own. We tried his method, followed it to the letter despite misgivings. After checking that Sophia wasn't hungry, her nappy was clear, and she was safe. We settled her into her cot. She was having none of it. We let her cry for several hours, crying ourselves as we forced ourselves to wait. She didn't let up. Eventually we couldn't take it anymore. Sophia was so beside herself that it took hours to calm her down. Sean took the book, ran into the garden, and threw it over the back wall into the open field.

'What a crock of shite,' he said. 'We'll never do that again.'

Our Sophia was not one to give in. Thank God.

At five months she could sit in a highchair. She presided over the kitchen like an empress, banging a plastic kitchen spoon on her tray, demanding attention, exploring the art of drumming. Nervously, we started feeding Sophia solids. Given her surgery we were naturally worried.

We began with super mashed banana and pureed organic baby food in jars. I was allergic to dairy and gluten as a child, so we avoided those. I wish I could say I was an earth mother who made vegetable and fruit puree from scratch, but I was not. I was a working mother, trying to shoehorn this new element into a busy schedule. Despite my discussion with Annetta, and knowing logically that fresh was best, I wasn't yet aware of how processed foods, even organic, were denatured, compared to the real thing fresh from your garden, or a local farm. I would wise up after meeting Joanna Blythman, investigative journalist, and author, and reading her book, 'Swallow This: Serving Up the Food Industry's Darkest Secrets' and reading Robyn O'Brien's book 'The Unhealthy Truth'.

We emerged from our first forays covered in food, like camouflaged agents ready for battle, except the battle had passed. In the battle, aeroplanes, birdies, and bumble bees, were deployed. Sophia looked quizzically at me as I buzzed. She was already familiar with the sound in utero, from practicing *bhramari pranayama*, bumblebee breath, in my yoga classes with Wonder Woman. I realised why babies wore large plastic bibs instead of old-fashioned cloth ones.

Sophia ate puree with no apparent problems and enjoyed most of them. We felt deep relief. A few days into the process she rejected a jar, was having none of it. My heart raced. Was her oesophagus causing a problem? I opened a different one. I took a spoon and buzzed the new offering towards her. She tasted suspiciously then swallowed and smiled, eager for the next one. I buzzed spoonfuls in, relief flooding through me. After cleaning up the war zone, I tasted the rejected jar and realised why she wouldn't eat it. It was horrible. We struck it from the shopping list.

By the time Sophia and I visited Dr Murphy for her 6-month paediatric check-up, she had settled into crèche, and we were both at ease. I squeezed Sophia's buggy into his cramped consulting room, backed onto the same parking lot as I had looked onto from the Domino birthing room. Sophia sat on my knee as Dr Murphy looked at her file. He pointed to the consulting table indicating where to place her. She looked suspicious but gave no major signals of dissatisfaction.

'How's Sophia doing?' asked Dr Murphy as he rolled her over to check the surgery scars.

'Great,' I said. 'She's very healthy.'

He tapped her in various places, then prodded or palpated others. I felt like leaping up to stop him.

'Are you still breastfeeding?'

'A little, but I'm winding down now I'm back at work.'

He rolled her onto her other side. We talked about how she was handling her initial pureed baby food, with glee and no problems. Dr Murphy was happy. He passed her back to me and sat down to write his notes. I cuddled her, then started to buckle her into her buggy.

Looking up I asked, 'How often do you see this malformation?'

'Not very often. We had one a few days ago. At home, I was telling my daughter about it, and she asked if the baby was a boy or a girl. I was quite surprised to find I didn't know. I try not to attach myself to patients, so I remember them as their medical condition.'

He didn't need to say any more. We both knew we were one of the lucky ones.

'And you still can't say why it happens?' I asked.

'No, it's a malformation like many others that we can't explain. It's not hereditary, that's certain. Perhaps it comes from lack of oxygen at a critical moment, or exposure of the mother to something toxic during pregnancy, we just don't know.'

'So, there's no risk that it will happen again if we have a second child?' I asked.

'I don't know of anyone who has had two children with this malformation,' he replied.

I made a mental note to tell Sean. We had discussed that two children would be ideal, as they would be there for each other, but we wouldn't be overpopulating the planet, just replacing ourselves. Now the idea of a second child frightened me. Even though Sophia's malformation was not hereditary, a similar thing could happen. The labour experience was also fresh in my mind and not one I was in a hurry to repeat. Having a baby is a risky business as we had discovered. The birthing of new life was not as simple as modern baby advertisements made one think.

The crèche was a short walk from my office so I could keep breastfeeding. The routine of going to feed Sophia was a great way to keep my connection with her, but I got the feeling the crèche didn't really want me to do it. They said they supported the idea, but when I was there to feed Sophia, I felt like I was in the way. They had often given her a bottle just before I arrived. Between the difficulty of getting the timing right, and feeling unwelcome, I soon stopped. With no more mother's milk antibodies, Sophia caught every cold going, and each one turned into an ear infection. Her start in a sterile hospital environment hadn't set her immunity up as well as Brigid's 'pick it up and eat it' approach.

Our doctor prescribed antibiotic after antibiotic. I started a spreadsheet to track exactly how many she had prescribed and what they were. When we reached six, almost back-to-back, I showed her. She was surprised. It was scary to me that she hadn't been tracking it, and that reminded me once more, why, as patients or parents, we needed to take notice and action in medical circumstances, not sit back and rely solely on the experts. Our GP booked us an appointment with an ear, nose and throat specialist. While waiting for the appointment, Sophia had two more infections, and the antibiotics necessary to stop them. We were getting worried. When we saw the specialist at last, we expected him to recommend swift intervention. Instead, he said, 'Wait six months, if she gets another one, we'll look at operating. If she doesn't, we'll leave it.'

We moved Sophia from the highly populated city centre crèche, to a neighbour who was a qualified child carer. Perhaps the word 'operating' kicked Sophia's immunity into gear, or perhaps it was being out of crèche; whatever it was, the next six months were infection free.

We had transitioned from hospital to home and onto the next phase of me being back at work. Sophia was healthy and happy, she loved being with our neighbour Trisha. Our lives took on a new rhythm as a family of three.

CHAPTER SIXTEEN

Second time around

Sean sat on the garden chair with delicately peeling green paint, and I on a blanket with Sophia. It was Saturday afternoon, spring sun warmed us and lit up new growth in the garden. The fig tree's first tentative leaves were like luminous green fairies dancing in the breeze. Sophia was a year old and finally sleeping through. She could talk and crawl at speed. We adored her. My Oxford friend Bev's deepest love was manifest.

'I don't want Sophia to be an only child,' I said.

'But are we ready to start the past year over again, the broken nights?' asked Sean.

Unaware of our momentous discussion about her family universe, Sophia saw a bug in the grass and motored towards it. The bug flew off just in time.

'We know the ropes now. It'll be easier,' I said. Amnesia about the pain of labour and the first couple of months of hormonal chaos had already kicked in.

'Maybe we should wait a little,' said Sean. He remembered more clearly.

'I'm thirty-five. We can't wait. Remember what I said about risks escalating.'

'What about Sophia's oesophagus?' asked Sean.

'Dr Murphy said he'd never seen it happen twice to the same parents.'

'Because they were so scared, they didn't have any more kids after that.'

We both laughed. He was joking but there was a ring of truth to it. We were fearful, but we also didn't want her to be an only child. Sophia crawled back to me.

'Mummy,' she said, looking up at me with her beautiful blue eyes, then snuggling in to hug me. I felt like my heart would burst with the love I felt.

That was all it took. We tackled our new mission with enthusiasm, and success was swift. Sophia was fourteen months when we discovered I was pregnant again. This time things were easier in every way. I ate organic food and avoided kayaking and other potentially dangerous sports. Like the first time, saying no to wine wasn't difficult. My body told me to stay off wine, coffee and garlic. As with Sophia, I had terrible nausea.

Despite my somewhat traumatic labour and birth experience, I trusted the Domino midwives at the National Maternity Hospital. I went back to Holles Street and was delighted to find that many of the midwives were the same as with Sophia. With their familiar faces I felt safe.

Instead of going to a yoga studio, I did yoga at home. Sophia and I needed to work on balance. She had started walking like a drunkard. She wanted to do it on her own like everything else. Her favourite saying was 'Fia do it.'

After she dived out of the front door onto the concrete, creating a massive graze down her face and confirming the neighbours' doubts about my mothering capabilities, I insisted she hold my hand.

With yoga, I encouraged her to follow my motion in cat cow. She crawled underneath me. We tested out tree pose, one side, then the other, laughing, both as unstable as students after a night in Temple Bar. When I stretched into puppy pose, bum up, arms outstretched, it was an invitation to play hide and seek. I lifted my head and said boo. We lay on the ground, her taking happy baby pose naturally, small hands gripping small feet in the air, me struggling to grab mine. Websites recommended flying a toddler on your knees in chair pose. I stared in horror, like I had when Senan threw Millie. I could not imagine taking such a risk with my precious daughter.

Sophia learned to speak early for her age, but walking came late. We should have been doing more throwing to give her confidence with equilibrium. We set a bouncing seat between the door jambs, and she spent hours singing and bouncing in the safety of it. Sean started a gentle flying practice. Lying on the ground he gripped Sophia under her arms and around her chest and flew her over his body, keeping her tightly gripped, his belly available as a soft landing below. As her balance improved, he started a different flying lesson, with her seated on his feet, arms stretched forward hands holding his, strictly no freestyle throwing into the air.

With a full-time job and a toddler, the pregnancy flew by. Sophia loved Trisha, the childminder next door. I started maternity leave and even though I was home, Sophia went to Trisha to keep her place. I rejoiced in some free time and began drafting a children's book. I had always wanted to write books.

We played the waiting game past the due date again. Our ninth wedding anniversary was four days past D-day. Sean took a half day so we could go for lunch to celebrate. Sophia was with Trisha so we had a peaceful romantic afternoon to ourselves. I planned to deploy all the methods I knew of to hurry the birth along and avoid induction via oxytocin drip. I booked a restaurant that had a curry option, and checked my stock of raspberry tea.

We followed the coast road to Dalkey so we could enjoy the views. On Coliemore road, the car began to judder. At the spot where we paused for the view of Dalkey Island the day we met our kayak instructor, it stalled. Sean tried restarting the engine. Nothing. I felt panic rising.

'Nothing serious. Don't worry Caro,' said Sean. He tried starting the car again, then looked up with a guilty grin. 'I think we've run out of petrol.'

My mouth dropped open.

'It's okay Caro. It's only a kilometre to the nearest station. I'll walk and bring back a jerrycan.'

'Feck, Sean! Imagine if we were racing into Holles Street and I was about to give birth. How could you run out of petrol at this moment in our lives? There's no way you are leaving me here, on my own, at four days past my due date. Feck. Imagine if I go into labour? They say the second labour can happen super-fast. What the feck. I can't believe it.'

We locked the car and started walking to Dalkey, me muttering short words beginning with f and Sean apologising. At the garage, Sean bought a jerrycan of petrol. He walked back to the car, and I continued into Dalkey village. At least there were people around if something did happen. I didn't relish the idea of my waters breaking on the street with no husband or transport in sight, but it was preferable to walking another kilometre in the cold.

Muttering to myself about irresponsible husbands, I waddled up High Street to the restaurant I had booked. I knew Sean had a lot on his mind, but this was beyond belief. What was he thinking? I ordered a fruit juice and tried to think calming thoughts.

By the time Sean arrived, I was serene. It was a gorgeous day; the car now had a full tank of petrol, and everything was going to be okay. The curry was excellent. By the end I was laughing about the experience that I would never let Sean forget.

Over the next few days, I kept checking the petrol gauge. Sean was onto it; the tank didn't drop below half. I felt antsy. I decided I needed a haircut and demanded that Sean do it. As part of our money-saving we had bought a barber kit and I cut Sean's hair. It was easy, a number two all over. A banker's cut. Cutting my hair wasn't quite so simple. I wanted it short. Sean hacked quickly while I distracted Sophia with kitchen utensils.

'Keep still,' he admonished as I leaned forward to take an offering proffered by our small, but very mobile, daughter.

'I'm hungry,' said Sophia.

'Hurry,' I said to Sean.

'I'm going as fast as I can,' he replied, hacking another chunk.

The result was short, uneven clumps. A 'fight with the lawnmower' cut that matched my mood. Edgy, uneven, liable to get ugly.

My contractions started ten days past the date pegged by the midwives. I timed them as Sean took Sophia over to Trisha, who had offered to be on call for the event. Sophia was excited about her sleepover, proud to be going to Trisha with her little overnight bag. She napped there on weekdays, so she was familiar with Trisha's cot. I watched them cross the street, Sophia's tiny hand in Sean's, the other holding Mia, her rag doll, a gift from Sean's mum and dad. Sophia was loving and caring. Mia was carefully stroked and put to bed on a silk cushion every night. It reminded me of how lovingly Kathryn had cared for Sophia in the ICU.

With the contractions timed just right, Sean and I drove into the National Maternity Hospital. The midwives placed us in a waiting ward of many beds. There were women waiting because they had health problems that meant they couldn't do the early labour at home, there were others starting the oxytocin drip that I had been subjected to. I took paracetamol and managed the contractions by intermittent standing, lying, and walking. Sean helped me count and acted as breathing coach. The contractions built slowly. With time to adjust, I was able to handle the pain.

I hit the boost button of the TENS machine at the peak of each contraction, greedy as a Labrador for its tingling sensation. TENS stands for 'transcutaneous electrical nerve stimulation'. A TENS machine sends mild electrical impulses to sticky pads positioned on the lower back. The electrical pulses stimulate the nerves running to the spinal cord and are thought to block the transmission of pain. I couldn't control the contractions, but I could control the little black machine in my hand. It gave me something to focus on and a false sense of power over what was going on in my body.

When the time between contractions met the limit set by the nurses, Sean went to let them know. They were at their shift changeover meeting. By the time the meeting was over and they came to move me, the contractions were rolling together.

As we walked up the corridor to the Domino room, I stopped every few paces to lean on the wall and breathe through the pain. The birthing room was the same physical place, but it felt smaller, cosier, and very different to the first time. Low lights were on instead of big fluorescent lights, and calm music was playing. By a miracle of rosters, Lara, the midwife who had been with us for the core part of Sophia's marathon birth, was on duty.

I started a circuit from wall to bed, leaning on each, in turn, as a contraction hit. Sean placed my overnight bag on a counter and rummaged for the essential oils and music we had selected. Music was already playing, and I was in no mood to start looking for my favourite tracks. As for the essential oils, we were already too far along for their lightweight relief.

Lara suggested breaking the waters to speed the birth up. I agreed. I was into any pain free way of hurrying things up. She took a long crochet needle and broke the membrane. Water gushed onto the soak pad Lara had placed on the floor under me. The contractions powered onwards. I kept walking between them and leaning against the wall or the bed when a contraction hit. I don't recall lying on the bed at all during the labour.

Moving helped but eventually I could take no more.

'I want an epidural,' I said.

'You're nearly there, Caro,' said Lara. 'Have some gas.'

I tried the laughing gas but found it as ineffective as I had the first time.

'Please, Lara! I want an epidural!' I said.

'The baby's almost here,' she said. 'You're doing so well.'

'I don't care! I want an epidural!'

'We're nearly there,' she said, ignoring my demand. 'You can do it, Caro.'

'Please, Lara,' I begged.

'You're doing so well,' she repeated calmly.

'Lara! I want an epidural now!' I shouted. If begging wasn't getting through to her, perhaps shouting would.

'There's no time for an epidural,' said Lara patiently. 'If I call for one, by the time the anaesthetist gets here, you'll have given birth. Caro, you really are nearly there. This baby will be born in less than twenty minutes. You can do this.'

Lara coached me and encouraged me. She told Sean what to do to ease my pain and to prepare for the imminent birth. Soon after she ignored my demands, I moved from the zone of extreme pain into a twilight zone. It was almost like a natural epidural. The major work of labour was over, and I was getting close. Perhaps it was also a matter of mindset. Lara had removed the option of the epidural from me, my body and mind had to deal with the situation. In meditation and mindfulness there is a concept of watching a painful feeling or sensation, not judging it, or fighting against it, then letting it float away. While I wasn't doing this consciously perhaps Wonder Woman's meditation teachings had left a trace in my subconscious.

I circled round feeling like a dog wanting to find the perfect spot to settle. Lara had laid a big sheet of white plastic on the floor. I felt the urge to push and followed Lara's instructions to squat down, holding onto Sean as I pushed. We tried that a few times with no result.

'You need an episiotomy. You'll tear if we don't, and it'll be worse than a clean cut,' said Lara. 'Are you happy for me to do it?'

'Do whatever you need to do,' I said.

Lara quickly gave me a local anaesthetic and snipped my perineum.

'Now we'll try it again,' she said.

I leaned back into Sean in a half-squat. Lara was positioned in front of me like a rugby player preparing to catch a pass. This time, when I bore down with the pressure, our baby appeared, first the head, then the body, like a slithery seal. Lara was ready, she made the perfect catch.

'It's a girl!' she exclaimed.

Lara clamped the umbilical cord, then Sean cut it. She wrapped our baby and handed her to Sean. I leaned in to look at our daughter and felt deep wonder and a sense of ecstasy. Perhaps the pain and giving birth without an epidural provided extra endorphins, whatever it was, I felt like I was high. My body continued the contractions and the placenta followed. The white plastic was covered in blood and afterbirth.

Sean passed our daughter to me, and I cuddled her feeling parental love, the deepest love, Bev's words that had contributed to starting our journey on the road of parenthood.

'Before you get too cosy there, I need you on the bed so I can suture the episiotomy,' said Lara.

I passed our girl to Sean, and he snuggled her while I got onto the bed so Lara could stitch the cut. Perhaps I was more focused on our baby, and the cut was smaller, but it felt totally different. There was no long black thread covered in gore. With the repair complete Lara wanted us to start breastfeeding as soon as possible. There was an urgency for all of us to know that our baby could. We settled her into my arms, and she latched on and sucked. This time I couldn't see the gold flowing into her, but I knew it was.

While I fed our daughter, Sean dug into my overnight bag for the book with our list of names. Like with Sophia, there was only one name on the long list that suited her, Elenna, meaning 'starwards' in Tolkien's Elvish language, quickly shortened to Ellie.

Freshly named Ellie soon tired of feeding and relaxed into my arms.

'Why don't you hop into the shower while we get her cleaned up and dressed?' asked Lara.

'Sounds good,' I replied. I passed tiny Ellie back to Sean, then walked over to the shower room. I felt like I had been for a good run but not much worse than that. I returned clean and relaxed.

'How was that?' asked Lara.

'I feel like a new woman. It was totally worth going through the pain without the epidural to be able to do that. You were amazing Lara. I could never have done it without your coaching.'

'Yes, you could have. You were ready for it. The other benefit of a natural birth is that usually you can go straight home, but given how late it is, the staff that could check you out aren't here, so you'll have to stay until tomorrow morning,' said Lara. 'Pack up your bag and we'll get you settled in a ward.'

This time I didn't need a wheelchair. I felt confident about having my baby next to me through the night. I could get up myself, there were no aftereffects of anaesthetic to hold me back.

Sean left around midnight. Back in Killiney, Trisha was awake and excited to hear about our new daughter. Sophia was fast asleep, so they decided to leave her to sleep through.

Ellie and I were worn out. We slept deeply. At first light her gentle snicker woke me. I picked her up and she latched seamlessly onto my breast. She fed peacefully. I changed her nappy, movements swift and confident. I snuggled her savouring the sensation of love, warmth, and wonder, at holding my newborn close. She was born at the same weight as Sophia, but she seemed so tiny. I had forgotten.

Feeling satisfied, safe, and comfortable, Ellie went back to sleep. I wondered if she was sleeping too much. I had no reference for a normal baby's pattern in their first two weeks. The nurse assured me it was totally normal. Newborn babies sleep most of the time, three quarters of it, to be specific. Sleeping almost constantly in the 24 hours after birth is normal. They are worn out after the hard work of birth, like their mothers are.

Breakfast was served. I ate undisturbed, then read my book as I waited for my taxi-man and his small accomplice. In Killiney, Sean collected Sophia, and explained that he and she were on an important mission to fetch me and her new sister, so we could all go home together. We had talked about Sophia's new sibling over the preceding months, but she didn't grasp the full import of what it meant.

Seeing them walking through the ward doors that morning, my heart filled with love.

'Mummy!' Sophia exclaimed, running to hug me. I clung tight and kissed her soft cheeks. Then I introduced her to Ellie, her new sister, in the cot at my side, fast asleep again after her second feed. As we stood beside Ellie, I felt a bond of love around us, like I felt when we first held Sophia in the High Dependency Unit. A photo Sean took at that moment shows a powerful glow around us, like a halo.

We had read that giving a gift from the new sibling to the older sibling was a good idea, so we gave Sophia a gift of a baby doll 'from her new sister Ellie'. She stroked the new doll, then placed it on the bed. She approached the cot and gently stroked Ellie's forehead.

She looked up at us quizzically. 'Hot dolly,' she said.

Sean and I held back our giggles, tears of love and laughter in our eyes.

We gathered my belongings and I held Sophia's hand while Sean carried Ellie to the car. This time, we knew exactly how to attach the baby seat. Seeing us installing Ellie in her old car seat, Sophia looked uncertain. As we took off, I looked back at her. She looked worried behind her tightly gripped toys, Mia in her left arm, and her new doll in her right. I don't think she realised that this sister was a gift for life. I felt concerned. Would we have a serious sibling issue?

For a few minutes after we took off, Sophia said little, her troubled face stark in the rear-view mirror. But as we hit the Rock Road, her face cleared of clouds, and she started chatting. The rest of the way home she talked at high speed in her usual way, telling us about the night with Trisha, her new sister Ellie, and her new doll. She had needed a few minutes of silence to process and accept her new sister. Ellie turned her tiny head to follow the sounds next to her, intrigued. It was the start of a powerful sister connection.

Mum arrived to help a couple of days later. Knowing my propensity for late births we had booked her arrival for two weeks after the due date. Wise. I prepared for broken nights and chaos with two children under two. But we were more experienced this time around. With Mum to help, and Sophia going over to Trisha for part of the day, we were ladies of leisure. We took long beach walks with Ellie, wrapped up for the cold of early spring.

When Ellie was a few days old we placed her in a reclining bouncy chair in the kitchen, with the extractor fan on, for her nap after dinner. She slept through ten hours. The bouncy chair and the extractor fan combined to create the ultimate baby sleep whisperer. We didn't worry about noise on the stairs or Sophia calling us, Ellie slept through it all.

Mum left and I felt at ease. This time I was okay on my own, I didn't descend into postpartum depression.

Annetta and I met up every few days to chat or walk on the beach. At her house, Sophia, Ellie, and I watched, stunned, and impressed, as her two boys flew around, knocking things over, fighting, or doing things Annetta had forbidden.

In our house, Ellie lay quietly in her bouncy chair watching Sophia play gently with her toys.

Annetta sighed. 'My house is never peaceful like this.'

We laughed. A few days later Sophia found the flour, and covered her, Ellie, and the kitchen, in it, proving our house could also be the scene of mischief. Sophia loved to play with the kitchen utensils. She put the outer ring from a tart pan on like a necklace and a peach-orange tea cosy on her head as a hat. She gardened with Sean, passing things to Ellie in her bouncy chair. I raced after her, lifting compost covered seedling trays, or lumps of earth, just in time, seconds before they went into Ellie's hands, and from there to her mouth. I'm sure some went in. Ellie's immunity was outstanding. She was getting the 'Brigid method' thanks to Sophia.

Sophia loved to take care of Ellie, to pick up her toys if she dropped them and give them back, or sometimes, to take a toy away, and replace it with another. Ellie took it in her stride. Sophia applied her phrase, 'Fia do it', to everything, including wanting to carry her sister. With Ellie sleeping through and Sophia going to Trisha for most of the day, my maternity leave was relaxed. Our lives found a new peaceful cadence as a family of four.

… CHAPTER SEVENTEEN

Follow your dream

Never one to languish in a peaceful state, I saw an advert for a vineyard in a French property newsletter when Ellie was five weeks old. Sean and I had dreamed of going wine farming and moving to France for years.

We put the dream into words a few years before when we lived in a rented apartment. That day, sheets of rain blasted in off the Irish Sea and splattered down the balcony windows, the drops moving like living things creating wild patterns on the glass. Beyond the windows, city lights reflected onto wet tarmac, and beyond that, dunes and wild sea disappeared into fog.

I was feeling restless. We had been in our apartment for a couple of years, and it felt like we were getting nowhere. I was making progress with my career, but we worked crazy hours and still didn't have enough money for a deposit for a place of our own. I enjoyed my work, but I couldn't say I was deeply fulfilled.

Cup of tea in hand, I sat down on the sofa with an 'O' magazine given to me by Aideen. As I browsed the stories, a framed message from Oprah jumped out at me. It went something like: 'Create your vision of where you want to be in five years. If you don't know where you're going, you'll never get there. Imagine everything, where you are, what you're doing, what you're feeling, who you're with, and write it down.'

I stared at the page for a moment. It was so simple and made so much sense.

'We have to do this,' I said, holding up the magazine to Sean.

'What?'

'Create our vision of where we want to be in five years,' I replied, passing the magazine to him.

'That's chick stuff, I'm not doing that,' he said, and handed it back.

I twisted his arm. Pen and paper in hand, we settled into opposite ends of the sofa facing out to sea. We thought for few minutes, then wrote, putting our souls into the exercise. When we exchanged our page of dreams, they were almost identical. We pictured ourselves on a farm in France, with vineyard and winery, gardens for self-sufficiency, and two dogs. We disagreed on many things, which made our matching visions even more incredible. We had discussed the idea in passing many times; Sean's grandparents were winegrowers. On a trip to France, we had fallen in love with the place and its vineyards, but we hadn't dared to take it further.

When we gave form to our dream that day, we didn't have the financial means to do it. We had no formal wine growing or winemaking education, no farming experience, and limited French. One could say it was an unachievable, impossible idea. But having written it down, we started planning for it. We created lists of things we needed to do to help it progress; wine classes, French classes, visiting France for research, saving instead of spending when it was a 'nice-to-have' or a luxury. We took tiny steps towards our dream, barely aware that we were. We were living Goethe's words. 'Whatever you can do, or dream you can, begin it. Boldness has genius, power and magic in it.'

Regardless of our long-term dream, I had needed a place to root. Two years after writing our 5-year vision, we bought the house near Killiney Beach. We tucked our France vineyard idea away, to prove like a good loaf of bread. Shortly after buying the house, my biological clock interceded after the weekend in Oxford. Sophia was born and her arrival focused us on family and health. Now that she was a thriving toddler and Ellie was safely birthed, our energy returned to pursuing our dream with even greater force. The property in the newsletter looked too good to be true. I forwarded it to Sean in excitement, then called the agent. It had just gone 'sale agreed'. We were gutted.

The more we thought about it, the more we wanted to make the move. We were both at a career turning point. Sean was ready for a change. We looked at other properties, but nothing came close to the one in that newsletter. A month later fate intervened, and the property came back on the market. Sean flew over to see it and we spent an intense weekend debating the pros and cons, then made an offer. We sold our house in Dublin in record time. The advert made our small semi-detached house next to a railway line and a sewage plant, sound like an exotic gem. The five-minute walk to the sea more than made up for the downsides. I would miss Killiney Beach. Andrew's fig cutting, now a lovely, small tree, was a defining feature in the description. The year before, one of the hottest on record, we had harvested ripe fruit from it. As a fig lover, I was sad to leave it, but I consoled myself that the farm in France was home to many fig trees.

That summer we packed up and prepared to change our lives from city professionals to winegrowers in rural France. Given the disruption we were about to put ourselves through, it was lucky that Ellie had become so attached to her bouncy chair that she wouldn't sleep in her cot anymore. She would kick her right leg just enough to get the bouncy chair going, and rock herself to sleep. She needed the skill of self-comforting, and the ability to sleep anywhere.

Even at a few weeks old she didn't suffer fools. She fixed the burliest of men with a direct stare that said, 'Mess with me and you'll be sorry.'

Trisha gave Sophia a pink cat soft toy as a farewell gift. Ellie fell in love with it and Sophia willingly gave it up for her baby sister. 'Kitty Cat' became Ellie's equivalent of Sophia's Mia. She would hug the pink cat, kick her leg, and off to sleep she would go, no need for anyone's help.

Sophia was a composed young girl except when it came to moving day.

'Don't take my chair!' she yelled as her highchair disappeared into the back of the van.

I explained we would see the chair at our new home in France very soon. I went through what we were doing, our plans for the coming weeks of transition. She nodded sagely. We had talked about it, but she had never known anything but that house on the quiet cul-de-sac where we had listened to Dr Kapur's voice over the mobile phone loudspeaker on the first terrifying day of her life as she waited to go into theatre for life-saving surgery.

It was our first home, the place where we felt settled for the first time in our married lives, where we had made the momentous decision to start our family, and where we had begun raising our daughters. We were leaving neighbours and friends. There were so many memories in it.

As we pulled away from the house for the last time, I cried like I had lost someone. Sean couldn't understand it. He offered consolation and promises of how wonderful France would be. But as we drove away, up Killiney Hill with the bay glittering in the distance, my tears continued to pour. Sean told me to stop because I was upsetting our daughters. I tried to, but I couldn't help myself. The emotion was far stronger than I anticipated. I knew I would miss our home, but I didn't expect this reaction.

'What's wrong, Mummy?' asked Sophia's little voice from the back seat.

'Oh baby, I'm sad to leave our home. I know our new house in France will be lovely, but I can't help being sad to say goodbye,' I said.

We arrived at our short-term rental and the demands of our two daughters and organising our nomad life took my mind off the sadness.

Almost five years to the day from our Oprah inspired visioning exercise, we moved into our new home in France, a vineyard complete with 18th century buildings and winery, with space for gardens for self-sufficiency, no dogs and two kids. Magic happened in the creation, the two dogs in our vision had transformed into two kids. Our dream wasn't impossible, it was 'I'm Possible'. The farm we bought was in liquidation. It was not the beautiful oasis we had imagined, but it had the potential to be.

Sophia started pre-school. Despite speaking no French, the first three days went remarkably smoothly. On the fourth day she began to sob as we drove into the school parking lot. We talked for a while, then she went bravely into the classroom, tears pouring down her little cheeks. I choked mine back as I got into the car, anxious not to upset Ellie, who was strapped in her car seat behind me. That afternoon, when I collected Sophia, she was in a good mood. She had had a great day with the teachers taking special care given her teary start.

The next day I expected another difficult morning. As we arrived, she announced, 'I'm not going to cry today.'

Her face was determined. I could see it was taking emotional power to keep it together. The same couldn't be said of me. Tears spilled as I drove out of the school parking lot. I spoke soothing words to Ellie so she wouldn't be worried. Her face in the rear-view mirror was unconvinced. She had a fine-tuned sense of what was going on, even at a few months.

Sophia didn't talk at all for the first couple of months of pre-school. The teacher voiced concern. We agreed to wait another month. Two weeks later when Sophia returned after the holidays, they couldn't stop her. Her French switch had turned on and blended with her Irish gift of the gab.

Our experience with Sophia's touch-and-go start to life had made us more ready to seize the day and move to France. We realised how fragile life was, and that we had to do what we envisioned, not sit in our armchairs dreaming. I didn't consider us risk takers, but the massive, life-changing move we embarked on, showed we were. Each of us is here to follow our unique dream. I don't know what makes one of us latch onto something and feel passion and purpose for it, while another passes by without noticing. Perhaps we are on a divinely guided journey.

A couple of years later, while I was washing her hair, Sophia asked me, 'Why did you leave me alone when I was first born?'

We hadn't talked about her birth, the time she was left in the ward, unable to swallow, experiencing her first shocking hours on earth, alone. She instinctively knew. I felt culpable for her first night on earth spent next to the night nurses, before we discovered her oesophageal atresia, and for accepting that she went to Temple Street Children's University Hospital without me, once we knew.

As I washed her hair, my eyes traced the horizontal scar that ran across her right upper back. Prof. Puri's surgery was so fine, it was barely visible. A tiny circular scar slightly above it caught my eye. I wondered what it was, then realised, it was the chest drain point. I felt a deep tenderness, love, and gratitude that she was with us, that she had made it through those terrifying first days.

We chatted about what had happened to her. I explained the surgery and how it had saved her life. She gave me a sage nod, true to her name. I filled the jug and rinsed her hair.

She got up and I wrapped a towel around her and hugged her small body tight to mine. I felt like I would explode with the love. We had come so close to losing her.

That night I told Sean about Sophia's question. We wondered how she knew. We hadn't talked about her birth and surgery for years, but our eyes met, and we remembered it all. There was no need for words. The terrible moment when the paediatrician told us, the waiting for Temple Street to validate if it was worth operating, the hours of surgery, our vigil at the hospital, and the wonder that Sophia was healed when she passed the X-ray test. Like with grape harvest at our organic farm, it was the people we remembered, as much as the events themselves: the staff at the hospitals, the midwives, the ICU and HDU nurses, the doctors, Sophia's exceptional surgeon, our friends and family that supported us and Aideen's motivation and support of breastfeeding as I made my wobbly entry into motherhood.

The extreme experience with Sophia's birth made us celebrate living. It made clear what was important: love and family, home in its deepest sense. These things that vibrate with our animal core, our instinct. I reached my hand out across the table. Sean took it. Our eyes met in wonder that our daughter was with us as our hearts sang with gratitude for this miracle of life.

Epilogue

"*There are only two ways to live your life. One is as though nothing is a miracle. The other is as though everything is a miracle.*" Albert Einstein

Sophia was soon talking French like a native speaker. Despite this, in the early days, I worried that we had taken on too much, that the massive change would create scars for our kids, for us. Looking back, I see that we've come out okay. Time as a young family goes fast and savouring the journey is a primary joy. Walking to school with Sophia and Ellie was one of my favourite times, as were simple things like picnics, or family bike rides together.

After attending local schools in Saussignac and Eymet, Sophia moved to Bordeaux to complete her final three years of school. We saw her on weekends and holidays. There was no more walking to school together. I missed it. One rainy winter day, I saw a call coming in from her, and picked up, expecting a general update or a request to buy her Friday train ticket home.

'Hi Fia lovely,' I said.

'Hi Mummy. I've got a really sore tummy,' she said, her voice echoing slightly on my mobile.

'Oh, my *chéri*, I'm so sorry,' I said, my heart racing as it always did, at any sign of danger for my daughters. 'What does it feel like?'

My mind flew around considering what it could be, and what to do, given she was an hour and a half drive away.

'It's like a burning sensation.'

My brain worked through what it could be. Appendicitis, gastro? Danger for my kids generated overdrive in my unconscious body. Sean was usually the one to handle crises. I tended to overreact, even get angry. It was a response I knew I had to control, one that I had learnt from my dad. I tried to calm my racing mind.

'Where is it?' I said.

'In my upper tummy.'

'How long have you had it?' I asked.

'A couple of days,' she replied.

'Do you need to come home?'

'No, I think I can make it to the weekend.'

She didn't seem concerned enough for me to hit the panic button. My heart rate inched back towards normal.

'Are you sure, my lovely?' I asked.

'Yes Mummy, I'll be okay. I've got to go.'

'Call us if it gets worse, or if you decide you need to come home,' I said.

'Okay.'

'I love you, Moot.' I had continued the family tradition of nicknames. Sean joked that I had more than a hundred for my daughters.

'I love you, Mummy. See you on Friday.'

I hung up and sat down for a minute, to breathe, and let the worry pass. Sophia was boarding because there were no local options for the '*option internationale du baccalauréat*' (OIB) she wanted to do. She had grabbed the independence and was thriving, 'Fia do it'.

Friday evening, I collected her from Gardonne train station. After giving her a hug, I asked about her tummy ache.

'It's still there, but not as bad as it was,' she said, between chews of gum.

'Show me where it is.'

She lifted her hand to an area below her right breast, exactly where the surgery had taken place. I still didn't think of her oesophagus.

'Perhaps you should stop chewing gum. Could that be giving you a sore stomach?' I asked.

'I doubt it, Mum. But I'll stop to see if it helps.'

The weekend was uneventful. Sophia returned to school on Sunday. Mid-week an email from a stranger on the other side of the world popped into my inbox. She said she was reading my first book about our lives in France, 'Grape Expectations', and loving it. She remembered being part of a prayer circle that had prayed for Sophia. She was so happy to read about her in my book. I felt gratitude flow through me.

Sophia returned from Bordeaux for the start of the holidays, and we settled in for a quiet evening together as a family. A fire glowed in the newly installed wood burning cooker and the Christmas tree was decked in red and gold. Aromas of fried homegrown onions, potatoes, and kale filled the air. As Sean put the finishing touches on supper, conversation turned to Sophia's stomach-ache.

'I haven't had the pain since I stopped chewing gum,' she said.

'That's great news,' I said. 'I wonder what it was?'

'When you chew, your body prepares to receive food, so your gastric juices start to flow,' said Sean. 'Your oesophagus moves to get the expected food down and the entrance to your stomach opens to let the food in. Perhaps if there is no food coming down, the burning sensation is because some acid from your stomach has escaped up.'

'OMG Fia! That's why you had the sore stomach. It's the gum. With your delicate oesophagus, you can't risk chewing gum. No gum ever!'

I felt a rush of memories of baby Sophia, of Prof. Puri drawing his fine web of stitches that provided the bridge over which the two ends of the oesophagus would grow together. I looked her in the eye and repeated firmly, 'No gum ever, Fia lovely!'

'Okay, Mum, okay, don't worry about it,' said Sophia, in her best Michael Rosen voice, dissolving my angst with our shared laughter. If you haven't already experienced it, look up Michael Rosen reading his poem 'The Car Trip'. LOL. Every parent has been there.

Sophia had transformed from a dependent newborn into a confident young woman. Her International Baccalaureate was specialised in American literature. Since she started it, we had re-read books like 'The Great Gatsby', and I had discovered works like 'A Streetcar Named Desire', and 'Intimate Apparel', for the first time.

There was literature and writing in the family. My great grandfather was a journalist. Sean, an English major, had worked as a journalist for almost a decade and was a booklover. Soon after we moved to France, Sean stopped reading. Something clicked out of place. He couldn't stomach it anymore. All the books he tried turned him off. Then a literature amateur who worked as a Washington DC advocate by day, and a podcaster by night, rekindled Sean's will to read, with his 'History of Literature' podcast. Sean waited for Jacke Wilson's Thursday podcasts like a child on Christmas morning. Between Sean's rediscovery of books and Sophia's studies, our family interest in literature was reignited.

That evening, after dinner, I gave Sophia one more reminder not to chew gum ever, then she, Ellie, and I, cleaned up. Ellie selected the music. We sang and danced between packing the dishwasher, wiping down, and cleaning pots. Doing chores together felt intimate and good. My happiest moments were doing everyday things together, harvesting, cooking, cleaning, folding washing. Doing these things alone wasn't fun. It was being together, the community, and shared experience, that made it fun.

Sophia looked for a family film to watch and found the story of Charles Dickens told through his creation of 'A Christmas Carol'. The film was partly biography of the life of Dickens, and partly the story of 'A Christmas Carol'. When Dickens was twelve years old, his father landed himself, his wife, and Dickens' younger siblings, in debtor prison. Charles was left to fend for himself. At twelve years old, he was considered grown up enough to earn a living and was placed in a workhouse. The experience helped shape his social conscience and perhaps provided impetus to his literary genius. 'The Christmas Carol' story about Scrooge and his ghosts of Christmas past, and Dickens' personal story, were reminders of the importance of love, friends, and family; three things we had learnt about on our journey into parenthood.

On Christmas Eve, we returned to a family ritual, which was to read a short story or poem, an original we had written specially for that night. I wrote a light-hearted escapade about our two cats, Sophia and Ellie wrote short stories from the heart, and Sean wrote a poem. The chewing gum incident brought Sophia's surgery and the months that followed it flooding back and Sean's poem picked up the thread.

The Coronavirus lockdown hit. I noticed small things more than before. The aroma of the grass when I lay down on it. The texture of the earth when I planted out Sean's lettuces. His tanned, sinewy arm, and work-roughened hand that passed the seedlings to me. My daughters' perfect skin, and the softness of the air, as we raked cut grass.

Easter weekend, Ellie, Sophia, and I, were in the kitchen, making bread, sipping tea, chatting, hanging out. Sean brought fresh spinach from the garden and cooked up brunch, eggs on freshly baked bread, fragrant as a flowering meadow. As we cleaned up, we danced, flapping kitchen towels like flamenco dancers.

Sophia's traumatic start reminded us to celebrate life. The Coronavirus pandemic made us revisit what was important again, helped us see beauty and joy in simple aspects of our lives. It reminded me to cultivate gratitude every day, to slow down.

Sophia finished school and was accepted to study a double degree Irish Law and French Law. She moved to Dublin for the first two years of the programme at University College Dublin, better known as UCD. There she reconnected with people from her early years. Aideen, her adopted aunt and fairy Godmother, became her home away from home. Millie, Brigid's daughter, became one of her best friends. Circles of life played out all around us.

Enchantment is everywhere if we just lift our heads to look for it. As Einstein suggested, 'everything is a miracle', the star-studded night sky, an apricot dawn, rain falling on soft ground, seeds pushing life out of soil, hugging a friend or a tree, shared laughter between lovers, a neonatal being healed, and a personal favourite, dancing with daughters.

Acknowledgements

A memoir is a personal journey, a way of making sense of the past, so my biggest thank you goes to my family, Sean, Sophia, and Ellie, for supporting me in sharing this intimate portrait of an intense moment in our lives. Sean says I write great fiction.

Special thanks to the people who were part of this adventure Aideen Dunne, The Domino Community Midwives of the National Maternity Hospital, Dr Murphy, the Temple Street Children's University Hospital, and Professor Prem Puri.

Thank you to our families: my dad and mum, Cliff and Lyn Wardle; Dad Feely and beloved Mum Feely, who is watching us from above; our siblings and their families. Thank you to our friends that are part of this story.

It takes time and a team to create a book. Thank you to my beta readers Dave and Patricia Smith, Annie Jefferies, Philip Hallworth, Alexsandra Horvat, Avril Miller, Frances Hook, Therese, Sean, Jeanne Wissing, Nicola Cook, Dawn Foster, Bobbi Heath, and Elke. Special gratitude to Alexsandra for her detailed suggestions. Thank you to Julie Adams for her patience and effort with the cover design.

Finally, thank you, dear reader, for reading my books. Thank you also to readers who have written to me over the years – your emails and letters provide great motivation to keep writing.

Why did the Oesophageal Atresia happen?

We don't know. It could have been lack of oxygen when I capsized on the kayak. It could have been the bleed I had at seven weeks. It could have been exposure to pesticides or plastic in my food or drink. It could also be multigenerational effects of systemic pesticides. We don't know which of these, if any, were responsible.

My recurring nightmare about my baby sinking down into the water was a premonition. Perhaps my body knew that Sophia's abnormality came from the kayak incident and hence the terrifying drowning scenc that I kept experiencing again, and again, in my dreams.

We know that breastfeeding made a difference to Sophia's recovery. I also know that since we have made a priority of eating fresh organic fruit and vegetables as a family, we rarely get sick. Us being there for Sophia, and our families and friends, being there for us, also helped her recovery. My wish for this story is that it makes a difference, that it encourages people to breastfeed, to eat organic and avoid pesticides, especially when pregnant, and to be there for friends that are first time parents.

Additional resources:

Nicola O'Byrne, who features in Chapter 14, offers online courses and support for breastfeeding at www.breastfeedingsupport.ie

Bliss Charity for babies born premature or sick https://www.bliss.org.uk/

TOFS lifelong support for those born unable to swallow www.tofs.org.uk

Research has shown that the herbicide glyphosate generates birth defects in the 3rd generation of lab animals exposed to it, see Kubsad, D., Nilsson, E.E., King, S.E. et al. Assessment of Glyphosate Induced Epigenetic Transgenerational Inheritance of Pathologies and Sperm Epimutations: Generational Toxicology. Sci Rep 9, 6372 (2019). https://doi.org/10.1038/s41598-019-42860-0 .

Despite what we know herbicide use is increasing rather than decreasing: https://chateaufeely.com/herbicide-growth/

A letter to you, Dear Reader

Thank you for reading 'Saving Sophia'. If you enjoyed reading it, please consider posting a review on your favourite book review site, or Amazon, or Goodreads. Reviews make a major difference to the visibility of a book. Thank you.

My vineyard memoirs 'Grape Expectations', 'Saving our Skins', 'Vineyard Confessions' and 'Cultivating Change', offer a glimpse of Sophia's life in her school years.

I invite you to visit www.carofeely.com and to join my mailing list. If you are part of a book club, page over for a list of book club discussion questions. I would be delighted to join your group via a virtual group call. We can organise to ship Feely organic wine to most parts of the world, so if you're a wine lover, you could have a wine tasting as part of your book club meeting. Email me at caro@carofeely.com

Following our dream to France was a passionate journey. Feely vineyard (www.Chateaufeely.com) is an award-winning organic estate with two Best of Wine Tourism Gold Trophies in the greater Bordeaux region and a Gold Trophy winner in the national wine tourism awards. The wine school and gourmet wine tours and walking tours in Bordeaux and Southwest France can be found at www.FrenchWineAdventures.com. We would love to see you here.

With best wishes and hugs, Caro

Book Club questions

How did the book make you feel? Were you already familiar with pregnancy, birth, and breastfeeding, shared in this book? If yes, how did it resonate with your experience? If no, has it changed how you engage with friends or family going through these phases of life?

What was your reaction to the story about Caro considering abortion?

Since this story took place, Ireland has legalised abortion. What do you think this means for the safety and support of women faced with an unwanted pregnancy?

Caro talks about speaking up with your intuition in the face of medical specialists that are offering their view. Have you experienced this feeling?

Have you ever had a premonition? Do you think the recurring nightmare Caro had in the weeks before the birth was her subconscious trying to tell her about Sophia's abnormality?

Which part of the book stood out to you? Are there any quotes, passages, or scenes you found particularly striking or thought-provoking?

Is this book different from the books you usually read? How does this book compare to other books you've read in your book club?

Did this book change you? Did you learn something you didn't know before? Has your behaviour changed?

Grape Expectations

Book 1 of The Vineyard Series.

What does it take to follow your dreams?

The wine filled my mouth with plum and blackberry sensations. A picture of a vineyard drenched in sunlight formed in my mind. Sean drew me rudely back to our small suburban home.

'How can they be in liquidation if they make wine this good?'

When Caro and Sean find the perfect vineyard near Bordeaux their dreams of a new life in France are about to come true. They arrive, with a toddler and a newborn, to face a dilapidated farmhouse, and challenges including accidents with agricultural equipment, cultural misunderstandings, and money worries. Undeterred, they embark on the biggest adventure of their lives – learning to make wine from the roots up.

Reviews

'A beautifully written tale of passion and guts.' Alice Feiring, Author

'Captivating reading' Destination France

'An inspiring story of how one couple changed their lives.' Jamie Ivey, Author

'I was delighted by this book, by what it says about the passion of winemaking, France, family life, and the challenges that build a marriage.' Martin Walker, bestselling author of the Bruno, Chief of Police series

E-book ISBN: 978-2-9586304-1-6
Print Book ISBN: 978-2-9586304-0-9
By Caro Feely

Saving Our Skins

Sequel to Grape Expectations. Book 2 of The Vineyard Series.

**'Earnest and winning... sincere and passionate'
The New York Times**

*'We have to get to the next level, or we have to get out,' I said.
'We have to have more vines and more accommodation,' replied Sean.
Both would take investment we didn't have.*

For Caro and Sean, building their vineyard dream and overcoming challenges that include a devastating frost, bureaucracy, and renovation setbacks, will take courage, ingenuity, and luck.

This book is about love and taking risks while transforming a piece of land into a flourishing organic vineyard and making a new life in France. It explores the reality of following your dream, challenges of building a new business, renovating in France and raising a family as a working mum; and includes nature, delicious food and wine, and voyages to Napa and Sonoma wine regions in the USA, and to Alsace, Bergerac, Bordeaux, and Burgundy wine regions in France.

Reviews

'So impassioned that it could inspire you to drop all security, move to the backwaters of France, and bet your life, all for the love of making wine.' Alice Feiring, author and wine writer

E-book ISBN: 978-2-9586304-3-0
Print book ISBN: 978-2-9586304-2-3
By Caro Feely
First published in 2014.

Vineyard Confessions

Book 3 of The Vineyard Series. Initially published under the title 'Glass Half Full' in 2017.

How do you balance a growing business and family life? Is it possible to have it all?

'Hand harvesting was different to machine harvesting. It was convivial and slow. We started at dawn and proceeded across the vineyards. It was better for us and for the grapes, the human scale and pace of it was peaceful and joyful. It gave us time to share confidences and confessions.'

But this rose-tinted glimpse of Sean and Caro's French vineyard life is only part of the story – with it come long hours and uncertainty. The rollercoaster ride of managing a growing business and navigating menopause is as challenging as making natural wine in harmony with the environment.

In this book you will discover the joys and challenges of living your dreams; navigating life changes, why organic matters and what organic wine, biodynamic wine and natural wine are.

Join Caro on her search for balance in love and wine.

Reviews

'A love story poured beautifully.' Robyn O'Brien, bestselling author

'Caro Feely is a force of nature! Caro draws the reader into her world with its all of its challenges, triumphs and heartaches. Required reading for winelovers everywhere.' Mike Veseth, author of Wine Wars and The Wine Economist blog

'Honest and touching. Caro Feely gives us the real thing including why we need to heal our soil and change the way we farm.' Martin Walker, bestselling author

'A brave and compelling tale' Alice Feiring, author and journalist

E-book ISBN: 978-2-9586304-5-4
Print book ISBN: 978-2-9586304-4-7
By Caro Feely
Retitled, edited and republished in 2023.

Cultivating Change

What will it take to change? Can we resuscitate our relationship with the earth? And with each other?

Cultivating Change follows the emotional journey of Caro and Sean as they regenerate their vineyard in France and rewrite their love story in the face of climate change. The book explores family dynamics, work life balance, yoga, organic farming, food, and personal awakening.

Join Caro as she searches for wisdom to address the climate crisis and to breathe new life into a stumbling marriage in this powerful new memoir.

Key themes: Primary themes: Climate change, Marriage, Wine, Vineyards, Organic farming, Regenerative farming, Biodiversity, Yoga, Personal awakening.

Secondary themes: Seasonal Affective Disorder (SAD), Raising teenagers as a working mother, Transitioning to the empty nest, Gastronomy, Expat living, Voyages to France, South Africa, Japan, and Italy.

Reviews
'Powerful and inspiring' Jacqui Brown, Book blogger
'A must read. Passionate, challenging, and informative.' Helen Melser, Author
'A thoroughly enjoyable read and a wake-up call about how our actions affect our planet.' Tora Shand

Print book ISBN: 978-2-9586304-6-1
E-book ISBN: 978-2-9586304-7-8
By Caro Feely
Published 15 June 2023.

Reviews of Caro Feely's books

Praise for Saving Sophia

'A heart-warming and deeply moving memoir of love and family that will touch every parent,' Martin Walker, bestselling author

'Beautifully written... I couldn't put it down.' Jacqui Brown, Book blogger

'Caro Feely writes with heart and soul. Saving Sophia is a visceral, deeply personal testament to motherhood and the village it takes to raise a child,' Fiona Valpy, Bestselling author

Praise for Cultivating Change

'Powerful and inspiring,' Jacqui Brown, Book blogger

'A must read. Passionate, challenging, and informative.' Helen Melser, Author

'A culinary trip with layers of biodynamic farming, secrets of nature, environmental activism, family dynamics, and resilience all tied up into a gorgeous package.' Kelly Ryerson, Glyphosate Facts

'I have heard it said that time changes things, but sometimes you have to change them yourself. In Cultivating Change Caro Feely confronts both sides of this saying, adapting to the effects of time on family and relationships, while simultaneous seeking to shape the world – especially the wine world – to meet the challenges of the future. Insightful and inspiring.' Mike Veseth, The Wine Economist

Praise for Vineyard Confessions (previously Glass Half Full)

'Honest and touching. Caro Feely gives us the real thing, not only living the dream of making great wine in France but the work required while raising a family and holding a marriage together, but why we need to heal our soil and change the way we farm.' Martin Walker, bestselling author of Bruno, Chief of Police series

'Caro Feely is a force of nature! Caro draws the reader into her world with its all of its challenges, triumphs, and heartaches.' Mike Veseth, The Wine Economist

'Vineyard Confessions is a love story poured beautifully onto the pages by Caro Feely. If you love wine or someone who loves wine, you will drink in every page of this book.' Robyn O'Brien, bestselling author

'A brave and compelling tale about a gnarly life in the vines and the choices we frail humans make in our emotional journeys.' Alice Feiring, author and wine writer

Praise for Saving Our Skins

'Earnest and winning... sincere and passionate' Eric Asimov, New York Times

'So impassioned that it could inspire you to drop all security, move to the backwaters of France, and bet your life, all for the love of making wine.' Alice Feiring, author and wine writer

'Should be required reading for anyone who loves wine! Even a teetotaller will drink up every page of Saving Our Skins, for the fascinating behind-the-scenes of organic farming.' Kristin Espinasse, French Word a Day

'Caro has produced a beautifully written sequel which in turn seduced and terrified me about the prospect of owning an organic vineyard in rural France. I thoroughly enjoyed the urgency of her writing – I needed a rather large glass of wine when I'd finished. Bravo, Caro.' Samantha Brick, author and journalist

'Saving Our Skins entertains and informs as it tells the story of her family making organic and biodynamic wine in the south of France. Required reading for wine lovers everywhere.' Mike Veseth, The Wine Economist

Praise for Grape Expectations

'Captivating reading for anyone with dreams of living in rural France.' Destination France

'Really liked Caro's book! Definitely the best – and most realistic – tome coming from the 'A Year in Provence' genre.' Joe Duffy, Irish radio personality

'Bright, passionate, inspiring, informative and absolutely delicious' Breadcrumb Reads blog

www.ingramcontent.com/pod-product-compliance
Lightning Source LLC
LaVergne TN
LVHW040003200726
843493LV00005B/1109